JACOB'S WELL

A TWISTY CHRISTIAN MYSTERY NOVEL

ANGUS REID MYSTERIES - BOOK I

URCELIA TEIXEIRA

AWARD WINNING AUTHOR

JACOB'S WELL

A TWISTY CHRISTIAN MYSTERY NOVEL

ANGUS REID MYSTERIES BOOK I

URCELIA TEIXEIRA

Bible scriptures were quoted from both the King James Version and/or the New International Version of the Bible. (Copyrighted worldwide as public domain)

Copyrighted material
E-book © ISBN: 978-1-928537-86-1
Paperback © ISBN: 978-1-928537-87-8
Published by Purpose Bound Press
Written by Urcelia Teixeira
First edition
Urcelia Teixeira
Wiltshire, UK
https://www.urcelia.com

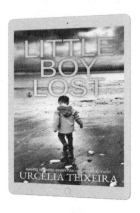

TO MY SON,

NEVER FORGET HOW MUCH I LOVE YOU.

As you grow older you will face many challenges in life, just do your best and keep

your eyes on God.

He's got you!

Life isn't about waiting for the storm to pass, it's all about learning how to dance in

the rain.

Every day may not be good, but find something good in every day.

Laugh, love, live, and listen.

Follow your dreams, believe in yourself, and live with purpose.

I'll always be with you.

LOVE YOU FOREVER, MOM

INSPIRED BY

Jesus answered, "Don't you know me, Philip, even after I
have been among you such a long time?"
John 14:9
(NIV)

PREFACE

A mother knows. At least, that's what everyone told her. That she'd know when something was wrong. Feel it. Deep inside as if there was an invisible cord that had stayed behind the day she brought her son into this life.

Well, they were wrong. Dead wrong.

She didn't know her son at all. But then, he didn't know her either.

CHAPTER ONE

The rhythmic ticking of the clock on Jake Foley's nightstand slowly picked at his nerves as he waited for his parents to go to bed. He had been lying in his bed for hours, biding his time in the stillness of the night. He stared at the full moon that streamed in through his bedroom window. Waiting had never come easy to him. A trait his mother always said he got from her. But this was one time he had to be patient—he couldn't risk getting caught. Not tonight. There was too much riding on it.

The house was quiet and from where he lay on his bed, he stared at the narrow gap beneath his bedroom door, looking for any signs that his parents might still be awake.

His dad, stepdad, in fact, was one of the church elders, and when on occasion their pastor couldn't deliver the sermon and the duty fell on his stepdad, he would often stay up late to work. But Jake had checked the family calendar on the refrigerator earlier that day, just to be sure he was not preaching that Sunday. His mom was good at keeping the calendar up to date and that gave him the peace he would be in the clear.

In the next room, his younger brother would be fast asleep too. Teddy was his stepbrother but he had never thought of him as anything less than the brother he had always wanted. Jake was only seven when their parents married. Teddy was three. There were only four years between them, at least double that since the car accident that claimed the life of Teddy's birth mother when he was just a few years old. And although Teddy had survived the near-fatal crash, the accident had caused too much damage to his brain. Teddy's neurons were no longer firing properly and by the age of eight, he'd regressed in age, keeping him from stringing more than a few sensible words together when his thoughts got stuck in a loop. That was happening more often as he'd gotten older but for the most part, Teddy was easy to be around. The part that wasn't as easy, was the constant care he needed. Care that had over the past ten years left its mark on his parents' marriage and slowly drained most of their savings—and Jake's college fund.

As Jake's thoughts ran away with him, doubt suddenly tugged at his emotions and he shoved it aside before it persuaded him not to go through with his plans. His mind was telling him he had to. He had no choice.

He turned to see if it was time to go yet, straining to read the old-fashioned clock's hands in the dark. Quarter past two. Close enough, he thought and gently peeled away the bedcovers. Picking up his worn red Converse sneakers with one hand, he slowly inched toward his bedroom door. There was no need to change; he'd cleverly gone to bed in his black hoodie and dark jeans.

The floorboard creaked just as he got close to the door and he bit down on his lip and froze in place. He stood there for a short while, listening. When it seemed the coast was clear, he opened his door and carefully popped his head around the corner. The house was quiet. In his parents' room at the end of the short, dark corridor, his stepdad's peaceful snores gave him the all-clear and he gently shut his bedroom door behind him.

Tiptoeing toward the front of the house, he passed Teddy's room and briefly glanced sideways at his bed. Only to find his thirteen-year-old brother sitting upright, his eyes staring directly at him.

"Can I come too, Jacob?" These days only his family called him by his birth name.

Jake's insides turned as Teddy called out to him and he glanced back over his shoulder to see if his mom had woken up.

"Shh," he said placing his forefinger over his mouth. "Go back to bed, Teddy."

But Teddy wouldn't have it and already had one leg swung over the side of his bed.

Jake's heart jolted as he took two leaps toward his brother.

"No, Teddy, go back to sleep."

"Why not? Why not?" Teddy's mind had gone into a loop, precisely what Jake had feared might happen.

Jake pinched his shoes under one arm and tried pushing Teddy down into his bed but Teddy's pleas got louder.

"Everything is fine, Teddy. Just go back to bed, okay? Heroes need their sleep, remember?" Jake forced a smile, hoping it would console his brother enough for him to go back to bed.

"I want ice cream," Teddy said, still louder than Jake would have preferred but at least Teddy had somehow found another distraction.

"Fine but keep it down. You're going to wake mom up and then you can forget about getting any ice cream."

Teddy mimicked the gesture to be quiet.

"Stay here. I'll go get you some ice cream," Jake whispered. "And if you keep this all secret, I'll add some of those nice chocolate buttons on top."

Visible in the soft glow of the moonlight, Teddy's big eyes stretched even wider as he nodded. Guilt and shame set into Jake's conscience. It was a big secret to keep for a thirteen-year-old, much less when he had the mind of an eight or nine-year-old. But he had no other choice given the circumstances and, if he didn't hurry, he was going to be late.

Dropping his shoes on the foot of the bed, Jake quietly hastened to the kitchen. He snatched the tub of Ben & Jerry's from the freezer, tucking it under one arm as he reached for the chocolate buttons and a spoon. He couldn't be bothered scooping it into a bowl; there wasn't time. So, he dashed back to Teddy's room. Jake dropped the tub into Teddy's lap where he was now quietly rocking back and forth in his bed, his small head light now in place above his brows.

"Here, but don't eat it all, okay? We don't want you waking up with a tummy ache. Hide the tub under your bed when you're done. I'll put it back in the freezer later."

It seemed to satisfy Teddy's untimely craving and with a near crisis now safely averted, Jake picked up his shoes and snuck off down the passage.

By the time, Jake had managed to successfully sneak out of the house and leaped off their front porch, his heart was pounding inside his chest. He was late. That could cost him everything.

With no time to spare, he pulled his shoes on mid stride as he headed across the front lawn toward the small woodland footpath a little farther down the street. The front of their house bordered a narrow patch of dense, leafy trees that were hedged in by thick shrubs on all sides and the path would take him through to where his ride would be waiting for him at the other end. At least, he hoped Aaron would still be there.

The cold winter air cut across his cheeks and he pulled his hoodie over his head. Fresh, salty ocean air mingled with the scent of the surrounding earthy foliage filled his nostrils as the wind pushed at him from the front. "Please be there," he murmured, sending a hazy cloud into the cold air. He ran the path in half the usual time, shooting out between the tall bushes on the other end of the residential woodland.

As agreed, Aaron's slick white BMW was parked up just ahead.

"You're late!" Aaron yelled as Jake dropped into the front seat next to him.

"Yeah, I know. I had trouble getting out of the house."

Aaron's foot flattened the accelerator, leaving his car's wheels to screech as he pulled away.

"It's not just your life on the line here, Jake, it's mine too. Do you have any idea what it took me to pull this off? I vouched for you, you know."

"Yeah, I know, sorry."

With Aaron's annoyance now at bay, he snuck a quick sideward glance at Jake from behind the wheel.

"Where's your *skims?*"

"My what?"

"You're gonna need a ski mask, dude. Trust me, you don't want these guys to see your face."

Aaron's words left Jake cold. He hadn't thought of

that. Why didn't he think of that? What if someone recognized him? Weyport was too small for him to go unrecognized.

"Chill out, dude. I have a spare." Aaron popped his chin out toward the glovebox and turned the car's nose toward the old highway that ran along the coast.

CHAPTER TWO

Roughly two miles outside of town, Aaron turned his car off the highway onto a narrow road that wound between the sand dunes toward the beach. The car slid sideways as the wheels hit a thick, sandy patch in the road, adding to the tension that already sat heavy in Jake's stomach. Where he watched the headlights beam across the grassy dunes, Aaron suddenly slowed the car down.

"Put it on. The skims," he clarified when Jake stared at him with a blank face, then, slipped his own mask over his head with one practiced hand.

Lacking Aaron's finesse, Jake did as Aaron said and pulled the black ski mask with the small red dragon embroidered on one side over his head. The fabric was thin and felt just as ridiculous as the stretchy fabric of his school wrestling suit. His mother thought joining the wrestling club would add bulk to his stringy body. She was wrong. It made him look like a dork instead. Uncomfortable with the mask over his face he tugged at it, eventually giving up after it made no difference at all.

"You'll get used to it, dude. The first time is always weird," Aaron said, leaning across to reach into the glovebox from where he took out a large silver kitchen knife Jake had somehow missed seeing earlier.

The blade glistened past Jake's nose before Aaron buried it inside one of his sleeves. When Jake stared at it a bit too long, Aaron was quick to notice.

"Chill, dude. It's just in case. I told you. These guys mean business. One can never be too relaxed around them. I never come here unprepared." He paused when he saw that Jake was still tense and unsettled next to him, then added, "It's too late to back out now, dude. Time to put your big boy pants on. Trust me. I've been where you are. If you want to make a lot of bucks fast, this is the easiest way. Just let me do all the talking and everything will be cool."

Jake nodded even though he suddenly wasn't so sure about it ever being cool. Nothing made sense to him anymore. How did he even get caught up in this? He and Aaron were scarcely friends. Had it not been for Aaron sitting behind him on the school bus every day, he would have never so much as spoken a single word to him. Aaron was a second-time-around senior with a bad reputation. And he, a junior with good grades who had never so much as gotten a speaking to since he first set foot in kindergarten. He had never done anything like this. Never needed to. But his stepdad was right. He was seventeen now. He needed to grow up and stand on his own two feet. If he wanted to help his family and go to college, this was the only way.

THEIR CAR PULLED up to a small clearing conveniently tucked behind a large sand dune where about a dozen other cars were parked. Some of them were even more expensive than Aaron's and Jake couldn't help but stare at them as they parked up.

"One of those could be yours soon, dude." Aaron elbowed Jake. "Didn't I tell you there's big money to be made?"

"Is that why you're able to afford this car?" Jake asked with caution.

"Yep, except I can't be telling the world about it so keep it to yourself. I pretend it's my dad's to avoid any suspicion on me." Aaron changed the subject and pushed his chin out to show him a luxurious black sedan.

"That's the boss's car, Moses. He bought that with cold, hard cash, and that's just one of them."

"Impressive." Jake paused. "Is the guy's name really Moses?"

Aaron made a snorting sound, the mask tracing the outlines of a wide grin.

"No way, dude. No one goes by his actual name. He

picked the name for himself. Said he was leading us to the Promised Land or something. I guess you'll know more about these religious things than me. Your old man runs the church, doesn't he?"

Jake didn't correct him.

"And for the record, don't call me Aaron in front of them. Around here my name is Dragon." He lifted his sweatshirt to reveal a large dragon tattoo across his chest. "I had it done from my first cut, as a reward, you know."

He didn't know, Jake thought. Getting a tattoo had never been on his list of rewards.

"I don't have a name," Jake responded instead, to which Aaron quickly replied, "That's easy, man. At school, we all call you Sasquatch, after that time you came to the school costume dance trying to look like Chewbacca. You looked hilarious, dude. Talk about a costume gone wrong. That's part of the reason why I picked you. You're a total geek. No one will ever suspect you. Now let's go. We're already late."

Mortified by Aaron's insulting confession, his cheeks flushed with embarrassment, Jake watched as Aaron jumped out of the car. He would have liked to tell him how much he hated his comment but there was no time. Instead, he got out of the car and hustled after Aaron where he had already started down a sandy footpath. The path wound between the grassy dunes to where it eventually stopped at the beach. After another minute's jog along the shore toward the river mouth, they pushed their way through dense water-lined foliage to where a houseboat quietly bobbed in the calm water.

As they drew closer to the boat, Jake could barely feel his legs beneath his scrawny body. He looked nothing like Aaron, all ripped and beefy like an All-Star quarterback. If these guys wanted to they could snap him in half like a toothpick. He wanted to pray, ask God to protect him but how could he? God wouldn't approve of this. Why would He protect him?

With shaky knees, Jake soon found himself inside the boat next to Aaron, tightly flanked by about two dozen more people. All, except one guy with some seriously crazy hair who stood in the middle of the room and about five others directly behind him, wore ski masks or other types of face coverings, some of them color-coded, some of them wearing custom logo jackets. Gangs.

The guy with the crazy combed-out Afro-looking hair wasn't from there. He'd know if he saw someone like that in Weyport. He looked Mexican, or perhaps Cuban. He couldn't be sure. His frizzy hair was a brownish-blond like it had been bleached by the sun and his clothes were casual as if he had just come back from a surf. Although his eyes were hidden behind red-tinted Aviators, Jake knew he was definitely older. His stepfather's age. He could tell by the gray stubble on his face. And judging by the way everyone stood like diligent minions listening to the guy go on about loyalty and teamwork, it was evident he had to be this Moses guy Aaron had mentioned.

They hid at the back of the small crowd, hoping not to draw any attention to themselves.

But Moses had noticed and he stopped mid-sentence, his eyes now fixed on the two latecomers.

"You're late," he said, his voice surprisingly calm; almost friendly but with a definite chill to it.

Aaron delivered a short, contrite apology, mimicking that of a soldier to his sergeant. Was he scared of this guy? Aaron McGee who strutted around school as if he owned it. The same Aaron who used to steal everyone's lunch money and somehow got away with it.

Moses summoned them with one long, curly finger on which he wore a wide, unembellished silver ring.

Dragon swore under his breath and yanked Jake by his sleeve. Singled out, they stood silent in front of Moses as his eyes ran up and down Jake's body, settling on his bright red sneakers before he looked up at Aaron.

"Is this the new guy?"

Aaron confirmed with a simple, "Yes".

Moses' eyes were back on Jake.

"Do you have a name, kid?"

"Jay... Squatch." Jake quickly corrected himself, choosing to drop the first part of the ridiculed nickname.

Moses smiled.

"Well then, *Squatch*. Even though I don't tolerate latecomers I'll let it slip this once, because you're new and Dragon is one of my best. But next time you're late, I'll throw you in the bear pit."

"Won't happen again," Aaron said, then turned and dragged Jake back to their spot.

"What's the bear pit?" Jake whispered to Aaron.

Aaron shot him a stern glance.

"You don't want to know, dude, but keep quiet. Moses doesn't like us talking when he's up there."

CHAPTER THREE

The rest of the meeting dragged on for another twenty minutes with Moses going on about up-selling and maximizing opportunities. Sounding much like one of his mother's boring Tupperware parties, it was clear that Moses was indeed as serious about his business as Aaron had said. At the point where it nearly became unbearable for Jake to listen to one more spiel about how there's no I in the word TEAM, Moses announced his speech was done and, as if a starting pistol had just gone off, everyone split into small groups. Jake followed Aaron to one of the groups where they were each handed a list of entries by one of Moses' unmasked men. No names. Just phone numbers. Next, they got given a small, black zipper pouch for which they had to sign a receipt with their call signs.

As soon as Jake got his, he pulled the zipper open to find a disposable phone buried among countless small plastic sachets half-filled with white powder. He drew back a sharp breath. There it was. The moment everything suddenly became real. The very instant he knew his life would never be the same again.

"You steal from me, Squatch, and you won't have the pleasure of seeing another sunrise."

Moses' voice was suddenly in Jake's ear and even with his ski mask covering his nose, Jake could smell the sharp aroma of onions on his breath.

Fear shot through Jake's scrawny body. Turning to face Moses, he simply nodded in response.

"Good. Dragon says you know your way around Weyport."

Again, Jake nodded.

"Business is picking up in the neighboring towns. I need to move my runners farther afield so I guess that's where you come in. Sheriff Hutchinson was instrumental in keeping things going around here and now that he's gone... well, let's just say my sales have hit a downward curve." He grinned, clearly enjoying the corporate metaphor.

"So, Squatch, Dragon tells me you are just the *man* for the job. Can I believe him?"

Jake wanted to say no, shout that he couldn't do it anymore, but he'd seen too much already. He'd never get out alive. So he just nodded again.

"Can I trust you?"

This time Jake managed to get the word out.

"Yes."

"Then, *mi casa es su casa!*" Moses stretched one arm out with a theatrical wave before he rested it on Jake's shoulder. "I have high hopes in you growing my numbers in this small town of yours, kid. And of course, you'll reap the rewards if you do it properly. Keep your head down and your mouth shut and we will get on just fine. Dragon will fill you in on the finer details."

His hand squeezed down on the back of Jake's neck as if Jake needed to be reminded not to cross the guy. Moses finished with a hard pat on Jake's back then turned and injected himself into another nearby small crew.

His commanding words lingered in Jake's ears long after Moses had left and it took every grain of courage for Jake not to turn and run for the dunes. Certain he had wet his pants he glanced down, thankful when he saw he hadn't.

"I got you, dude, chill. He can be a bit scary I know. But there's not much to this job. You call them up, always use the burner, agree on a time and place, and make the sale. The more you sell, the more you earn. It's that simple, man. Insider tip: always check your money. And oh yes, you get a bonus if you sell out before the one-week deadline." He winked, a broad smile shaping underneath the mask.

"And if I don't?"

"Dude, he takes it off your cut and adds it onto your next run. Compounding is what he calls it."

"But there's a lot of bags in this pouch," said Jake.

"Chill, bro! I've seen you around school. You're smart. I'm sure you'll figure it out. Time to bounce. My old man will knock me senseless if I'm not back to wake him up in time for work."

Jake frowned as they walked back to the car, pouches in hand.

"Your dad knows about this?"

"Heck, yeah, it's what pays for his liquor and gambling habits."

IT WAS NEARLY five thirty in the morning by the time Aaron dropped Jake off in the same spot he had picked him up. He was shaving it fine and he ran up the path to his house. His mother was an early riser and usually up by six a.m. He'd have to be careful of getting caught.

He held back behind the tall oak tree at the edge of the garden, checking first if the kitchen light was on. Satisfied that it wasn't, he proceeded with stealth across the front lawn until he reached the porch, the pouch still clamped in his hand. The house seemed quiet and he bent down to get the spare key from underneath one of the planters, now holding the pouch between his teeth. From the other side of the door, he heard shuffling and before he knew it, the front door was flung open.

"Jacob?" His mother's voice came at him.

"What are you doing out here so early, son?"

Jake snatched the pouch from his mouth and quickly hid it under his sweater behind his back, his insides trembling.

"Hi, Mom. I couldn't sleep so I came out looking for the newspaper. We have a school project coming up so I thought I'd get an early start."

He was rambling, he knew, but it was all he could think of at that moment.

He put the key back under the pot, desperate to hide his eyes. Even though half of his blabbered answer was the truth, his mother had the uncanny ability to sniff out his lies in an instant.

"And what's that behind your back?" His mother's eyes pointed at his back.

Another jolt shot through his heart.

"Nothing." He pulled his hoodie down over the small of his back.

She looked at him with suspicion but then stepped aside.

"Come on then. You're letting the cold air come in. And just so you know, the paper is never here before six thirty. I'm making your favorite breakfast though; oatmeal. Want some?"

Jake told himself to act normal.

"Sure, just have to feed my fish."

He darted past her. It was as good an excuse as he could come up with under the circumstances and as soon as his bedroom door shut behind him, his knees gave beneath his body and he collapsed onto the floor. As he knelt there on the floor, desperate to make sense of the emotions that ripped through his insides, his eyes fell atop his Bible next to his bed. Shame, guilt, anger, regret... he felt it all in one fleeting moment. He hated lying to his mother. Hated doing this. But he hated seeing his mother broke and stressed even more. He lurched himself toward his nightstand, snatched his Bible, and tossed it in the drawer of his nearby desk. Perhaps one day he could face God again, but not now, not today.

He willed his mind away from his self-inflicted condemnation and instead pulled the pouch out from behind his back and took out the list and phone. Searching around his room he soon found just the spot to hide the pouch. Another rummage around in his school bag delivered the sandwich bag with the leftover lunch he had taken to school the day before. Cramming the half-eaten cheese sandwich into his mouth, he shoved the black pouch inside the plastic bag, sealed it, and taped it to the underside of his fish tank's lid.

Feeling somewhat victorious that he had managed to escape being caught, he crammed the client list and phone inside his pants pocket and set off to find his mother in the kitchen.

He'd done it. He'd managed to find a way to help his parents with Teddy's bills and hopefully, a way to pay his way through college.

CHAPTER FOUR

A few days had passed since Jake received his first consignment. So far, it had been an easy job. Using the assigned mobile phone, he had sent a generic text to all the numbers first, introducing himself as their new contact and letting them know he had a limited supply of treats, as he put it. The FOMO tactic he had seen his mother use a thousand times before when she had a new product hit the Tupperware catalog, seemed to work like a charm, and within a few hours of sending the messages, the orders started pouring in. Excitement coursed through his veins with each new order. Perhaps he could do this after all. He had watched his mother many times before, often helping her prepare her orders before she went out to deliver them. Approaching his business in the same way she did made perfect sense. He had even photocopied one of her order sheets and used it to keep track of his. A genius idea he surmised none of the other runners could have possibly thought of. At one stage, he caught himself wondering if it would make Moses proud if he saw how resourceful he was. But just as quickly as his desire for approval came, the thought repulsed him and he shook his shoulders in reaction to it as a shiver ran over him. Why would he want to make Moses proud? The man was a criminal. A drug dealer who had already threatened to throw him in a pit and feed him to bears if he messed up. Why would he want his praise? What was wrong with him?

He shifted his focus back to the messages on his phone. He had decided to keep the drop-off point well within walking distance from his house since he didn't have a car, at least not yet. Once he had enough money, he'd buy himself a cheap one and put most of his earnings toward the medical bills and his college fund.

Recalling Aaron's warning words to make sure he got rid of his full batch before the next houseboat assembly, he staggered each meet-up with a ten-minute gap between each scheduled time; just in the event someone ran late. If everything went according to schedule, he should get through the batch in three days and well within Moses' deadline.

As far as he was concerned, he had thought of every-thing. He'd identified where the surveillance cameras were and where it was best to meet without being seen; on top of the small pedestrian bridge that ran over the river between the back of the church and the cemetery.

He'd even come up with a plan to dodge Teddy's new midnight ice cream craving by leaving a small tub in a cooler under his bed. They'd agreed to keep it a secret between them, between two heroes. At first Jake felt guilty about roping his younger brother in on his criminal activity, but then somehow he'd managed to convince himself that what he was doing was heroic. He was saving his parents from losing everything they had. That was a good thing, right?

TONIGHT THE MOON wasn't as bright. Perfect, he thought. It will help him stay unnoticed once he got outside. As before, Jake lay in his bed, waiting until his parents went to bed and the house was quiet. When he was certain they'd fallen asleep and his stepdad's snoring had once again given him the go-ahead, he snuck out of the house. This time with ease since Teddy hadn't woken up yet. It was one a.m. He had planned it perfectly.

Taking just what he needed to fulfill the night's orders, he had transported some of the contents from the black zipper pouch into his stepdad's travel pouch which he had dug out from the back of one of the drawers in his desk when he wasn't looking. Of late, they hardly traveled anywhere so he was certain his stepdad wouldn't even notice that it was gone. With it now safely strapped to his belly underneath his sweatshirt, he pulled his hoodie over his head, tucked his cold hands inside his pockets, and set off toward the church that was less than ten minutes walk from their house.

The neighborhood was dark and quiet and before long, he had made it to the bridge without any trouble. With his ski mask now covering his face, he kept his head down and waited for his first customer.

In the distance, he heard an owl, its hooting drifting on the thin layer of fog that hovered between the gravestones. He had never been out there at night and it was downright eerie, to say the least. But he told himself to keep his head. It was no different from being there in the daytime.

Thirty minutes went by and two of his customers didn't show. Were they just late, or had they changed their minds? Nerves suddenly bubbled up from the pit of his stomach. If he didn't move his product he'd face the bear pit; what that meant he still didn't know. All he knew was that he didn't want to find out.

He pulled the cell phone from his pocket and sent off a text to both customers. From somewhere behind him, a twig snapped and he spun around. At the foot of the bridge, on the cemetery side, a dark, lanky figure stood facing his way. Dressed in black clothes from top to bottom, a wool balaclava covering his face, he stood waiting with his hands in his pockets. Jake's heart skipped a beat. Keep it together, man, he told himself, simultaneously wondering if he was meant to make the first move. When he didn't, a gruff voice drifted toward him.

"You Squatch?" The guy asked.

"I am," Jake answered, desperate to not let his voice show his fear.

The man took a few steps forward, stopped to look around, then walked right up to Jake and held out the cash between his index and middle finger. It had caught Jake off guard and he stared at the cash.

"You got it or not?" The gruff voice came again, this time sounding a bit more aggressive.

Jake snapped back to the present and fumbled with the zipper of his travel pouch. When his lack of experience exposed the entire contents of his pouch, he suddenly realized he was at risk of being robbed by this guy. He wouldn't stand a chance against him. With numb fingers he pulled out a sachet, quickly dropping his sweatshirt back over the pouch.

"I'll have more next week," Jake said, hoping it would distract the guy from helping himself to his entire batch, even though he had no idea if he could make good on his promise.

But as soon as the exchange was over the guy turned and disappeared between the dark shadows of the gravestones.

Stupid! He told himself as he tucked the money inside one of the other sections of his pouch.

Before long, his next customer arrived and this time he was prepared. He had taken a few bags out ahead of time and kept them inside the pocket of his jeans. This he repeated as the night went along, topping up between each transaction.

By the end of the night, all but one customer turned up according to his carefully laid out schedule, which ran like clockwork. As planned, it was nearly four thirty when he slipped back into his house, sporting a grin so wide it hurt his cheeks. After he safely hid the cash inside his fish tank, he climbed into bed. Everything had gone according to plan. Aaron was right. It was an easy job. One he had managed to do without any trouble.

CHAPTER FIVE

Angus Reid pushed his chair back from his desk and lifted his cup of cold coffee to his lips. Becoming a sheriff had been all he strived to be ever since that fateful day. It's what was needed. To rid his guilt. To keep looking.

Every day, every endeavor, it had all built up to this moment. His perfectly crafted plan to pin the star to his chest so he could finish what he started all those years ago. He had made an oath to himself. Back when it happened, and now to the people of Weyport: fighting for justice, saving the helpless, and serving the people. Even when it had cost him his marriage. And now more than ever, he had every intention to make true on all of it.

He glanced down at the seven-point star on his chest. He should have been happier than ever. He'd achieved his goal and killed two birds with one stone when he took Pete

Hutchinson's post as Sheriff of Weyport while serving him the justice he deserved. But somehow, the joy he should have felt escaped him. Not because he was ungrateful or particularly disappointed in how it happened, but because for the last month, since he became the town's sheriff, he'd been discovering just how deeply corrupt Pete Hutchinson was.

He glanced at the pile of folders on his desk. He had pulled all the open case files dating back a year. Case files that should have been closed by now had Pete done his job properly. Case files that presented more questions than answers. Case files that were riddled with secrets and lies. Weyport was in trouble and he had no idea where to begin.

"Looks like you might need another cup there, Sheriff. I just made a fresh pot. Want some?"

Tammy Simmons' face beamed pure sunshine when she popped her head inside his office door.

"You must have read my mind, Tammy. I should have tossed this one hours ago. Thanks," he added.

She walked over and took the cold coffee from his hand.

"It's no trouble at all, Sheriff. I'll make sure you're taken care of." She flashed him a smile that nearly made him blush before she turned and set off toward the coffee machine.

Nearing her thirties, Tammy was a pretty girl. Tall and slender with big green eyes that she knew how to use to her advantage. But beyond all her beauty, Angus had so far mostly been impressed with her work ethic. She'd been the administrative assistant for the Weyport Sheriff's Office going on six years now and seemed to be well respected in and out of the office. If he was to clean up his town, he could do with a helping hand who knew her way around the office and townsfolk.

"Here we go. One fresh cup of *hot* coffee." She smiled again, handing him his coffee.

"Smells great, thanks."

She lingered, her eyes trailing the contents atop his desk.

"You sure you don't need help going through all these cases, Sheriff?"

Angus shook his head midway through a big mouthful of coffee.

"I think it's best I go through them myself, thanks. Helps if I see the information first-hand."

"Sure thing, Sheriff. Oh, that reminds me. Old Mrs. Richardson called again. She's insisting that she saw someone wearing a black face mask run past her house in the middle of the night. But I checked. We haven't had any reports of any burglaries anywhere in the neighborhood. Not even a triggered car alarm. What would you like me to say to her? She won't stop calling."

Angus scratched the back of his head.

"I'll take care of it. I'll pop around and show my face. Can't have one of the town's oldest citizens complain that the new sheriff isn't taking her seriously. Besides, I could do with the distraction."

"Good call. Mrs. Richardson is renowned for creating a stink if things don't go her way. I'll send her address through to your phone."

Tammy spun around and returned to her desk and barely a minute later, the message sounded on Angus's mobile.

THE FRONT DOOR to Mrs. Richardson's house was flung open the instant Angus pulled up in his brand new marked Durango. In her late sixties, her petite frame hurried down the garden path toward him.

"It sure took you long enough, Sheriff. If you want to be this town's sheriff you had better react a bit quicker. I could have been dead by now." She wagged her arthritic finger in front of his face.

Stifling his amusement at her admonishing as if she decided his fate as town sheriff, he greeted her.

"I'm sorry, Mrs. Richardson. I got here as soon as I could. Why don't we step inside and then you can tell me all about it?"

His words seemed to appease her and she turned and made for the front door. Once inside, she walked straight to the window, explaining that this was where she stood when she spotted the masked man walking down her street.

Angus pushed the delicate, white curtain to one side and peered out into the street before dropping it back into place.

"Do you recall roughly what time this was when you saw him, Mrs. Richardson?"

"Of course, Sheriff Reid. I made a note of it." She reached back to pick up a writing pad on the nearby dining table.

"See, here, four twenty-three a.m." She handed him the note.

"That's quite precise."

"Yes, it is. The clock is right there, see?" She pointed to the antique grandfather clock in the far corner.

"Indeed it is. May I ask if something woke you up? Why were you up so early?"

"I'm always up at four a.m., Sheriff. Every day for the past forty years. That's how I manage to keep my house in tip-top shape without neglecting my other duties. You should try it, Sheriff."

She was hinting at his tardiness.

"I'll take that to heart, thank you, Mrs. Richardson." He glanced back through the house.

"And Mr. Richardson? Any chance he saw the guy too."

"Oh, he won't notice a bear if it pokes him in the eye. Besides, he's not an early riser like me. He was lifting the rafters until nearly eight thirty. That's when he usually sits down for his breakfast."

"So he didn't hear or see anything." Angus double-checked.

She looked at Angus through squinted eyes.

"You think I made a mistake don't you, Sheriff? I can tell that's what you're thinking. I'm old, probably have bad eyesight, it's dark, yada yada yada. I might be old but I'm not senile. I know what I saw. Take it from me. I've been around long enough to know when something suspicious is going on in my neighborhood. And this guy was definitely suspicious. Who runs around with a mask on his head in any event?"

Angus couldn't deny her point.

"Yes, that does seem odd except we ran an incident report. There were no burglaries or breaking and entering of any kind anywhere in the neighborhood last night. Could it be that it might have been someone going for an early morning run and the light hit his face wrong? It's still pretty dark at that time and I'm assuming you would have had a light on inside the house then. That would make it a bit harder to see outside, especially if these curtains were still drawn."

He knew he was risking Mrs. Richardson's wrath but he needed to say it.

At first, Mrs. Richardson didn't speak as she now glanced out at the street.

"I suppose so," she said, the fire in her belly now somewhat subdued.

"Tell you what I'll do, Mrs. Richardson. I'll take your

advice and get up early tomorrow morning and I'll drive through the neighborhood myself on my way to work. I have a ton of work to get through anyway. Sound good?"

She nodded, her hands suddenly on his arm and the fire back in her belly.

"I made a fresh batch of granola cookies this morning. Wait, let me give you some."

She hurried to the kitchen and was soon back with a plate of cookies and pushed it into his hands.

"You have one of these with your coffee when you wake up. It'll give you an extra boost. It's an old family recipe full of goodness. Not this rubbish you young people put into your bodies these days."

Satisfied that her new sheriff was living up to her expectations, she ushered him out onto the porch from where she watched Angus drive off before she disappeared back inside her house.

CHAPTER SIX

Success tasted good, Jake thought as the last of his customers turned around and disappeared between the gravestones. He shoved the guy's cash inside his concealed belly pouch, now bulging with notes, and walked toward the church. Somehow, he had managed to sell out his entire quota in just two days. Something he thought he'd never be able to do. Could it really be that easy, he wondered. He'd never been this successful at anything in his life before. Even though he tried his hardest, his grades were average. He had long since accepted he was not the academic type. He didn't play any kind of sport either. Jake Foley was nothing but an average Joe. In every possible way. And although college was the next tier on the education ladder to success, he still had no idea what he wanted to study.

But the prospect of having his own little business

changed everything. This he was good at. This he did with hardly any effort at all. This made him feel empowered.

He kicked at a stone with his shoe when his conscience poked at his soul. Under ordinary circumstances, he'd thank God when things went right in his life but he knew full well this couldn't be one of those times. This he knew God would never approve of. Suddenly he knew exactly why Adam and Eve hid from God and he wondered if God would ever forgive him. As quickly as the thought came he ejected it from his mind. He didn't want to feel guilty. He didn't want to be thinking about his faith right now. Didn't want to face God. Surely God knew he was only doing this to help his family.

He shoved his hands deeper inside his pockets, tucked his chin into his chest, and set off through the churchyard. He wasn't going to do this forever. Just a short while, until he saved enough for college and settled Teddy's medical bills. He'd already decided how he would get the money to his parents without them knowing that it came from him. He would simply leave a church donation envelope with cash in their mailbox. Perhaps he would add a note that said it was to help with Teddy's bills. His parents would assume it was just another gracious church member's donation, except this time it wouldn't be coupons for food or clothing. This time it would be a fat wad of notes. The thought brought a smile to his face and he could almost imagine seeing the relief on their faces when they opened the envelope. And if business continued like this, there might even be a little extra for that holiday his mom had always dreamed of.

With a smile still etched on his face he felt like he was on top of the world. Finally, he was in a position to help them. Finally, his stepdad would see there was nothing average about him. And it felt good. Really good.

As he crossed the dark quiet street a block away from his house, his cell phone suddenly buzzed against his belly and he pulled it out from between the cash. Crouched down in the shadows of two trashcans that had been left for collection later that morning, he read the text message. It was from one of his customers from the night before. He was asking for more *treats*. This time double the amount he delivered the night before. Jake texted him back. Tomorrow he'd ask Aaron to take him back to Moses for another batch. He glanced at the time on his wristwatch. It had just gone four twenty-five. He was right on time.

TRUE TO HIS promise to Mrs. Richardson, Angus had set his alarm for four a.m., instantly regretting it when the shrill sound went off and yanked him from a deep sleep. He slammed his hand down atop the clock radio and groaned into the darkness. If he were a dishonest man, he'd turn around and carry on sleeping. Except he wasn't. He also knew that Mrs. Richardson would without doubt be standing at her window looking out for him driving by.

And having her wrath come down on him was the last thing he needed.

The sobering thought had him instantly awake. He flicked the covers off and swung his legs over the side of the bed, rubbing his palms across his face. It's only for today, he consoled himself.

Ten minutes later, he was dressed in his uniform, his thermos and two of Mrs. Richardson's granola cookies in hand. As he stepped out into the B & B's small parking area and walked toward his car, The Mill's signage flickered on and off above his head. Time to find a place of his own, he thought as he dropped the thermos in the cup holder between the seats and drove toward the center of town.

The entire town was still in slumber when he slowly drove the car down the three blocks toward Mrs. Richardson's street. Apart from the local bakery's lights being on, all the other shops were still closed. As he approached her neighborhood, he passed the church and decided to pull over in front of it. He'd been meaning to drive by to see what time the Sunday service started and now was as good a time as any. He rolled down his window and from inside his car scanned the poorly lit notice board out front. Making a mental note of the time, he paused when he thought he saw something move along the side of the building. With his vehicle lights now switched off, he sat forward in his seat and stared out into the dark space to where he could just see the edge of the cemetery.

Something was definitely moving in the distance and he looked at it with more intent. A second later a raccoon darted off across the street and soon disappeared into the nearby bushes. "False alarm," he murmured to himself and relaxed back into his seat before he slowly drove his car down the quiet road. Careful not to let the engine wake up the neighborhood, he gently turned up into one of the side streets, deciding to crisscross through the small neighborhood. The slow drive allowed him to properly survey the dark corners between each house as he passed them, scanning up and down each driveway. It seemed Mrs. Richardson was right. There was something so calming about being up before the rest of the world started their day. At this rate, he'd be behind his desk before sunrise, which would give him at least a three-hour head start before Tammy clocked in. More importantly, he'd gain the respect of one of Weyport's esteemed residents. Something he desperately needed if he was to gain the townsfolk's trust.

When he neared the street where Mrs. Richardson lived, he drove a little faster, suddenly eager to get to the office. From the corner of his eye, as he passed one of the side streets, he caught an odd-looking shadow moving next to some trash cans and he slammed on the brakes. He threw his car into gear and backed up until the spot came back into view.

CHAPTER SEVEN

As Jake got up from between the trash cans, tires screeched somewhere to his right. He looked up and saw the red taillights from a vehicle backing up fast. Under the glowing overhead streetlight, the markings on the car came into full sight. It was the new sheriff's car! He dashed back and hid behind the trash cans, his heart beating so fast he thought he was going to faint. Perhaps he didn't see him, he reasoned. But as soon as he saw the sheriff's car turn into the street, its headlights now on full, he knew he had been spotted.

Still crouched down behind the trash cans, Jake turned to find an escape route. If he could clear the fence at the end of the narrow alleyway that ran between the two houses behind him, he might be able to cut through Mrs. Richardson's garden. Out of time, he had to make his move.

To his right, the headlights were approaching fast, now aimed directly at the trash cans. Thinking he had better hide his face, he yanked his ski mask over his face and made a run for the fence behind him.

The car's tires screeched to a halt behind him. He ran. As fast as his scrawny legs that now felt like jelly would take him. When he reached the nearly six-foot high fence, he leaped onto it. His sneakers slid down and he was back on the ground. Adrenaline surged through his veins as his mind fought to find another way to clear the fence.

"Stop!" He heard the sheriff yell from somewhere behind him then heard his car door slam.

But Jake didn't stop or look back. His mind was working too hard to find an escape.

To his right, an empty planter stood atop a wheelbarrow and he reached to pick it up, hardly feeling the full weight of the clay pot as his body reacted to the surge of energy that pushed his muscles into overdrive.

The sheriff's feet slammed onto the concrete driveway behind him.

Jake dropped the giant planter onto the ground, hoisted himself over the fence, and slammed down the other side.

"I said, stop!" The sheriff's voice echoed into the darkness on the other side of the fence.

Jake's body was operating at maximum, his heart sitting tight in his chest. He sprinted across the lawn toward the slightly lower fence that separated this house from Mrs. Richardson's. This time it was much easier to clear the fence and he jumped into Mrs. Richardson's back yard. The garden light went on, blinding him for an instant. Shielding his eyes, he kept running and bumped into one of her wrought-iron garden chairs. Pain stabbed at his thigh but he kept running.

Behind him, Mrs. Richardson's fence rattled as the sheriff cleared it.

Jake pushed his body forward, still not looking back.

He burst through the small garden gate and ran out onto the front lawn before turning right to sprint the last few meters to his house. He had to hurry. Before the sheriff caught up and saw him disappear into his house.

One. Last. Sprint.

His feet slammed down on the sidewalk.

His lungs felt as if they were going to explode.

He pushed his body harder than he had ever needed to before.

Just when he thought he couldn't go any farther, he reached the bottom of his driveway. Ever so briefly he turned back to see where the sheriff was, relieved when he didn't see him.

Ducking underneath the low branches of the tree, he turned, ran across his front lawn, and leaped onto their front porch. The timber landing thumped loudly under his shoes but he couldn't worry about that right now and nearly exploded through the front door. Thankfully, he had left it unlocked behind him when he slipped out earlier. As he shut the door behind him, now a bit more cautious not to be making more noise than he already had, he heard his mother's whispers sound from their bedroom as she attempted to wake up his stepdad.

Yanking the ski mask off his face, he made one last stealthy dash toward his room. With mere seconds to spare, he slipped inside his room and quietly shut the door behind him.

It took less than two seconds for him to pull his shoes and clothes off before he jumped into his bed, the pouch of cash still strapped onto his body. He snatched a T-shirt off the floor, and pulled it on, wiping the beads of sweat from his face in the process before he pulled his bed covers up to his chin.

Outside his door, he heard his parents shuffling down the corridor to the lounge. Still out of breath, he lay very still, praying the sheriff didn't see him run inside his house. But his fears soon became a reality when there was a soft knock on the front door.

Jake wanted to cry. Wanted to scream. Or run. But he couldn't do any of it so he kept his emotions at bay and shut his eyes as tight as he could.

Moments later he heard his bedroom door creak open and sensed his stepdad's presence at his door. He froze. Lay deadly still.

The door quietly shut again and he heard his stepdad's voice announce that his son was sound asleep in his bed. That it couldn't have been him running through the neighborhood. That he was a good kid and that he'd be the last person on the planet to do something as stupid as that.

And as Jake listened and the sheriff left, he could finally breathe again.

When the house quieted down and his parents had gone back to bed, reality kept Jake up for the rest of the night. He had so nearly been caught tonight. Narrowly escaped the jaws of the law. Nearly destroyed his family.

And for the first time since he ventured down this dark path, Jake realized just how dire the stakes were. How risky his little business venture truly was.

But instead of heeding the silent warning, instead of listening to the small voice that cautioned him to turn away, Jake decided to continue. Because for the first time in his life, Jacob Foley felt what it was like to live on the wilder side of life.

And he liked it.

CHAPTER EIGHT

M ary-Jean Foley, or MJ as most people in Weyport called her, tackled her role in the church with vigor. As with everything she'd done in her life. In her mid forties, she was the proverbial Proverbs 31 woman: virtuous, strong, and selfless; character traits she was immensely proud of.

An early riser from as far back as she could remember, she didn't wait to be served but instead allowed her servant's heart to live her life tending to the needs of others over her own. It had become her purpose, the very thing that turned the cogs of her soul and gave her life meaning. But that was ripped away when her first marriage to Jacob's father tragically ended after he died of colon cancer. High school sweethearts, taking care of him and their baby boy, Jacob, was her entire life, her incentive for leaving some good behind on this earth. But when her first husband passed away and took along with him the very core of her being, she suddenly found her soul craving for more. Apart from the joy Jacob brought her, she sought new meaning to her life, so it then came as no surprise when she met Jacob's stepfather, Joe—short for Jonathan—that she was more than ready to become someone's wife again.

She met Joe in Portland at a single parents' grief-counseling group. They had both turned to it for help after tragedy plunged them into the single parenting sphere. Jacob had just turned four and showed signs of needing a father figure in his life. In turn, Joe's young mentally disabled son needed extra care. It was as if God sent MJ new purpose and not long after, MJ and Joe got married and once again, MJ's dream of having a family was realized.

Joe was a firm Christ follower and it was he that had led MJ to discover an entirely different purpose to life she had never even known existed. And for the first time in her life, serving Jesus was far more enriching than anything she had ever done before. It was as if she was created for that purpose alone.

So when the opportunity arose for Joe to help plant a new church in Weyport, the pair had no hesitation in accepting and MJ embraced all that serving the Weyport community had to offer with verve.

~

JAKE SQUEEZED into his usual seat in the front of the church. Next to him, Teddy was busy on his electronic doodle board, a nifty tool his therapist suggested they used to help focus his mind and keep him calm. From where they quietly sat waiting for the service to start, Jake watched as his mother moved from person to person like a frog jumping between lily pads in a pond. She was great at what she did, always smiling and making sure everyone was happy. In the opposite corner his stepfather and a few other elders stood huddled together, their hands atop Pastor Rob's shoulders as they prayed over him. His stepdad was a good man and had been a good father to him but in recent years, it seemed he was pushing Jake too hard. As if he wasn't doing enough. Wasn't who his stepdad needed him to be.

Jake turned his attention to the row of stained glass pictorials that were set in the walls on the far side of the church, his eyes settling on a picture of Christ. It was as if Jesus' eyes were looking directly at him. He shuffled in his chair and looked away. He had been attending church every Sunday since they first moved to Weyport, apart from the time he had chickenpox, and never once had he felt so uncomfortable as this. As he tried, to make sense of his feelings it didn't take long before he knew exactly the reason. It was because he had a secret. A secret he couldn't hide from God, even if he tried.

Several weeks had passed since he first started working for Moses and he'd made a lot more than he initially expected to. Since that second night when Sheriff Reid nearly caught him, he had managed to find a way around it, snuck in and out of the house more easily, and become more vigilant when he met up with his customers. He'd become crime smart as Aaron once called it.

Aaron had become somewhat of an older brother to him too and they hung out at the skate park nearly every day now. But in the last few days, Aaron had been acting out of sorts. As if he too carried a secret, one that even Jake did not know about.

All through the service, Jake's mind was everywhere but on the message or the worship. He had become numb to his surroundings, a master at pretending. He had to.

When the service was over and his mother dragged him into helping her at the coffee station, annoyance got the better of him.

"Why do I have to be the one who has to do this? Why can't someone else help for a change?" Jake asked as his mother dragged him behind the coffee station and immediately got busy with a cappuccino.

"Because that's what we do, my boy. We serve one another." MJ paused midway through frothing a cup of milk and looked at her son, a curious frown on her brows. "Is anything the matter, my boy? You seem a bit... off," she whispered directly next to him.

His mother's question caught him off guard and Jake struggled to find a suitable reply. So he did what most teenagers would do and lied, instantly feeling the guilt that settled behind the fib.

When he looked up, he met with Mrs. Richardson's piercing scrutiny. She held his gaze for what seemed like forever before, much to his delight, his mother's friendly voice cut through the palpable tension between them.

"Just the person I was hoping to see today," MJ said in her usual upbeat voice as she started pouring Mrs. Richardson a cup of tea. "Any news on who's been traipsing around our neighborhood, Mrs. Richardson? The entire town is talking about it."

Mrs. Richardson dropped a cube of sugar in her cup, swirled the tea around with a teaspoon then answered, her voice tainted with sarcasm. "Sadly, no, and no one has seen the thief since, so until our new sheriff proves his worth, I guess we'll be forced to bolt our doors at night."

As soon as the words left Mrs. Richardson's mouth, a man cleared his throat directly behind her, startling her so she nearly spilled the entire cup of tea all over the counter.

"Sheriff Reid!" MJ cut in. "How nice to see you here. I didn't know you were a churchgoer. But we're not complaining. It's about time our law enforcement was on the good team. Let me get you something to drink. My boy here makes the best cappuccinos, don't you, Jacob?" MJ's effervescent voice saved Mrs. Richardson's obvious discomfort but instead shifted all the attention now to Jake.

Panic rushed through Jake's body. Desperate to avoid

eye contact he dropped his head and got busy with the sheriff's drink.

"Happy to be here, thank you," Angus replied, then tipped his head at Mrs. Richardson whose cheeks were still flushed with embarrassment.

"Just a note of caution, Mrs. Richardson, we don't want to go around calling the man a thief when he hasn't actually committed any crimes. I think it will be best if we don't unsettle the townsfolk any more than they already are. I assure you, I've been patrolling the area personally, every night since we spotted him, and I am committed to keeping Weyport safe as far as humanly possible. Just as I promised you I get up at four in the morning." He finished with a polite smile to drive his point across.

Mrs. Richardson put her cup to her lips as if to silence her mouth from saying any more than she already had. From the embarrassed look on her face, it was clear she was desperate for the earth to swallow her whole.

"Of course you are, Sheriff, and we're so thankful." MJ came to her rescue once again then quickly changed the subject. "Say, Sheriff, I have a delicious tenderloin roasting away in the oven. How about you join us for lunch when we're done here? It's about time we properly welcome you to our town."

CHAPTER NINE

Sitting across from Angus at the lunch table, Jake kept himself busy with his plate of food. The less he said, the better, he thought. Even when his mother tried to include him in their conversation, he had made sure to stuff two large spoons of mashed potato into his mouth so he wouldn't have to respond.

"My you're a hungry young man today, aren't you, Jacob?" his mother commented before turning the conversation back to Angus.

"So, Sheriff, tell me, have you managed to find yourself a home yet? Our town doesn't have a huge supply of properties, you know? It seems someone has to either die or move away before a home comes up. Unless, of course, you're prepared to move into Hutch's old home. Although my guess is you might want to pass on that one." She gave him a warm smile.

"You're right. I'm beginning to realize that there's a short supply of housing. But, desperate as I am, I think the further I distance myself from the old sheriff's reputation the better. I've just extended my stay at the Old Mill and the ladies at Weyport Realty are keeping an eye out for something that comes up."

"Well, if you ever need a place to stay in the interim, you will be more than welcome here. As long as Jacob still fits on the couch you'll have a bed here." She winked at Jacob, hinting at his height.

Jacob coughed a chunk of mashed potatoes across the table, leaving both MJ and Joe rambling off their apologies for their ill-mannered son.

Jake and Angus locked eyes. He was certain the sheriff could see straight into his soul.

"I appreciate that, Mrs. Foley, thank you but I'm sure Jacob would prefer keeping his bedroom. Who knows what secrets he hides in his room?" Angus's voice was teasing as he smiled at Jake.

But Jake's heart dropped into his stomach. Having the sheriff stay at their house was the last thing he needed.

"Oh, that's so funny," MJ said. "I'm sure all moms say this but my Jacob is one of the good ones. He doesn't have a dishonest bone in his body. Besides, we're a close-knit family and we don't keep secrets from each other. It's not pleasing to the Lord." She smiled as she popped a forkful of lettuce into her mouth, her eyes reflecting honor and pride.

"I'm sure he is, ma'am. I didn't mean to imply otherwise. It's just that I was once a teen too and well, at around this age everything we do is somehow done in secret. Whether intended to be or not." Angus turned to face Jake, who to this moment still hadn't breathed a word, then he continued. "As long as you know you can always come to me if you need help, Jacob. Anything at all, okay?"

Jake forced a smile in response. "Sure, thanks," he forced out, gulping down half a glass of water to mask his discomfort.

"Can I be excused please, Mom? I have homework," Jake added, desperate to get back to the safe confines of his room.

"Of course, honey," MJ replied. "Perhaps you could also clean your fish tank today. It's starting to go green. Not that I understand why. The pump had been working just fine and then suddenly, wham, it stopped."

Again, Jake's heart caught in his throat before it dropped like a stone into his stomach when Sheriff Reid spoke.

"I had a large tank with a few tropical fish back in Nevada too. Unfortunately, I had to leave it behind when I moved to Millcove but I'm hoping to get another one once I'm settled," he said.

"Great! You know all about these tanks then. Perhaps our kind sheriff could have a look at that pump for you, Jacob."

Jake spluttered through his mouthful of water. "No! I

mean, I've got it, Mom, thanks. I'll clean it." Jake's reaction had his mom's eyebrows raised in curiosity so he added. "Besides, it's my responsibility to look after my fish, remember?"

Joe spoke for the first time.

"The boy's right, MJ. He should absolutely honor his responsibilities."

"So, can I be excused then, please?" Jake asked again to which Joe nodded in response.

"Clear your plate though, please," Joe added.

"I want ice cream," Teddy interrupted just as Jake got up. "Heroes need ice cream."

"Do they now?" MJ laughed. "And who are you saving, Hero Teddy?"

Jake's knife dropped loudly on his plate and the seemingly clumsy incident evoked irritation in Joe whose face made no effort to hide it. With his patience tested, Joe was quick to react.

"What's the matter with you today, Jacob? Do you have a test or something tomorrow that's making you so nervous?" He snapped. "I do apologize, Sheriff. Kids these days, huh? Off you go then you two. Your mother's been hiding some of that nice Italian ice cream in the chest freezer. She thinks I don't know about it but it's there." Joe winked at his wife. "She's a good wife this one. I've been trying to get a grip on my health and well, who doesn't have a weak spot for ice cream, huh, Sheriff?" Joe laughed.

Jake didn't waste one moment and he quickly disappeared into the kitchen with Teddy closely behind him. In the distance, he listened as his parents' banter soon turned to the sheriff's background and questions about how he intended on keeping the town safe.

Grateful that he had managed to escape the lunch unscathed, Jake settled Teddy in front of the TV with a large bowl of ice cream before he took up refuge in his bedroom.

He was certain the sheriff suspected something. Perhaps he did recognize him that night by the trash cans. Perhaps he came for lunch to properly check him out. Jake paced his bedroom, his nerves gnawing at his insides as he bit at his fingernails. When his gaze settled on his lime-green fish tank he darted across the room and yanked the lid off. One of the pieces of tape had peeled away from the lid and caused the edge of the black pouch to drop into the water and block the ventilation pipe that ran into the pump.

CHAPTER TEN

"No, no, no!" he said through a clenched jaw when he noticed that water was seeping in through the zipper.

He yanked it from the tank and dropped it on the ground in front of his tank, dumping the contents of the pouch onto the floor as he bit down on his bottom lip. He was as good as dead if he lost any of his stash. He sorted through the small plastic bags, pushing a few partially dry ones to one side. A few notes had gotten wet also and he gently smoothed them onto the floor before he dabbed at them with one of his dirty socks that lay on the floor to one side. His eyes fell on the stack of wet bags. They were completely waterlogged, their white contents now caked together to one side of each plastic bag.

He jumped to his feet, his fingers interlocked behind his head as panic rushed through him. Replacing these out of his own pocket would set him back thousands of dollars. Even if he took everything he'd managed to save thus far plus the future orders of his now regular customers, it would not be near enough to recover the stock loss. How did this happen? Why hadn't he been more careful, chosen a better hiding place? He should have known there was a risk of it getting wet. It was a fish tank for goodness sake! He kneeled down in front of the small pile of bags and tried squeezing out the water before he dabbed at them with his dirty sock. It was useless. They were completely spoiled. Worth absolutely nothing.

He pulled the burner phone out from inside one of his hiking boots, which he had hidden in the back of his closet, and dialed Aaron's number. The instant he heard Aaron's voice on the other end of the line he let rip.

"Dude, I'm in so much trouble right now. You need to help me. I've lost all of my bags, dude. I don't know what to do. If Moses—"

Aaron's voice cut in. "What do you mean you lost them?"

"They got wet. I hid the pouch in my fish tank and somehow it got wet. What am I going to do? We're talking thousands here! There's no way I can go to the meeting without this money. I'm as good as dead, Aaron!"

Aaron went quiet.

"Aaron? Are you still there? Did you hear me?" Jake's voice had gone up a notch.

"Yeah, yeah, I'm here. Leave it to me; I'll sort it out.

Flush them. I'll meet you as usual at the skate park tomorrow. I've got to go."

The line went dead before Jake had a chance to ask how Aaron was going to sort it all out. But then, perhaps it was better he didn't know. Aaron had been pushing for years. If anyone knew what to do it would be him.

With the phone now back in his shoe, he scooped the two unspoiled bags up and stuck them inside the sock before doing the same with the money. The fish tank was no longer a viable option so he hid the stuffed socks inside the nose of his hiking boots and pushed them to the back of the closet. A quick visit to the bathroom had him flush the worthless bags down the toilet, exactly as Aaron had told him to do.

He turned his attention to cleaning out his fish tank, wiping out any evidence along with it. Tomorrow he'd meet Aaron at the skate park and Moses would be none the wiser.

THE SKATE PARK was busier than usual and Jake chose to wait for Aaron on a bench in a corner farthest away from the main boarding ramps. He mindlessly spun one of the wheels on his board where it leaned up against his knee. He couldn't skate to save his life but acting the part played an important element in hiding his activity. He had never been one for skating, which was precisely why it had surprised his mother when he suddenly asked her to buy him a skateboard. Knowing full well that she'd be very eager to have him involved in any kind of outdoor activity, it was another one of those moments where his lies had compounded to the point where he stopped paying attention to the guilt that came along with it. It was as if it rolled off his tongue with no effort at all. Perhaps he'd gotten used to it. Perhaps he'd gotten good at it. Perhaps it was too late to care about saving his soul.

Never intending to actually use the board, he blended in perfectly where he sat waiting for Aaron on the bench under a shady tree. But try as he might, Jake was restless. Aaron was late, by now missing their usual five o'clock arrangement by more than an hour. Nerves started to gnaw at the back of his mind and he compared the time between his cell phone and his wristwatch. Six twenty-two p.m. There was no mistake.

Jake stared out into the distance. It wasn't like Aaron to be late. He was never late. Questions swirled around in Jake's head. What if Moses got wind of his mistake? What if, whatever Aaron was doing to help him, had put Aaron at risk?

Unable to sit any longer, Jake jumped to his feet, tucking the skateboard under one arm like he'd seen others do. He glanced around the park. There was still no sign of Aaron. Deciding to call him instead, Jake dropped back down on the bench and dialed Aaron's number. The phone just rang. Once more, he called this time checking that he'd dialed the right number. He did, except, now Aaron's phone didn't even ring.

Something deep inside his gut told Jake that something was wrong. Horribly wrong. Something must have happened. Aaron always took his calls.

Suddenly conscious of the possibility that Aaron might have gotten caught by the sheriff, or Moses, settled in his mind. If Moses had gotten hold of Aaron, it meant that he'd be in trouble too. By this time he knew just how ruthless Moses could be if he as much as sniffed someone was cheating him out of money. Especially this much money.

Jake flipped his sweater's hood over his head and scanned both park entrances. There was no sign of the sheriff or his deputies anywhere. Aaron had taught him how to spot the police or narcotics guys who worked undercover and wore plain clothes. No one looked even remotely suspicious. Nor could he see Moses or any of his men.

Just to be sure he wasn't getting ahead of himself, he called Aaron's cell once more. There was still no ringtone. Deciding he'd be foolish to hang around the park after dark, he got up and slowly moved toward one of the exits. He held his head down, not looking up or behind him once. Inside his body his heart drummed against his chest, increasing its tempo the closer he got to the gate. If either Moses or Sheriff Reid were there to take him down, they'd wait to do it outside the park, away from the other kids.

When he exited the park, his legs felt like two pillars of lead while in contrast, his insides were swirling out of control like a twister. From the corner of his eye, he spotted movement behind a nearby tree. A man, a large one at that, leaning against the tree was looking directly at him. Jake's heart stopped and he hastily changed direction. But as he walked away from the man at the tree he spotted another large man in the parking lot directly ahead of him, his beefy arms crossed over his large chest as he stood next to a parked black car waiting for something, or someone.

CHAPTER ELEVEN

R ight away Jake recognized the guy. It was one of Moses' men. He was certain of it. He stopped and stared directly at the beefy man's face. His suspicions were spot on. He'd seen the guy shadowing Moses a few times already.

Fear gripped Jake's throat. Whatever Aaron had done to help him out had now landed Aaron in trouble instead. And now they were coming for him.

Jake stood frozen midway between the two henchmen, weighing up what very few options he had. His mind raced in an effort to figure out how Moses even knew where to find him, or what he looked like. He'd been wearing his mask with every meeting and every drop. How was it that Moses came to know who he was? He brushed the puzzle aside. It didn't matter anymore. What mattered most now was that they had found him.

His mind jumped to finding a way out from under the problem. Perhaps Moses would understand if he explained the situation and if he promised to pay off his damages over time or he could work extra routes to make up for what he owed. Perhaps Moses just wanted to talk to him. For all he knew Aaron might even be in the car with him and everything was okay.

As Jake contemplated his problem, his eyes fixed on the black car beside the beefy guy. Moments later the window rolled down to reveal Moses sitting in the back seat. Their eyes locked and Jake drew in a sharp breath. Panic rushed through his body and he could no longer feel his legs, his heart now racing out of control as fear took a hold of him.

Hope clung to the back of his mind and he searched the space beside Moses, desperate to see if Aaron was with him. He wasn't. Instead, the unfriendly expression on Moses' face confirmed that he knew all about the cache Jake had lost.

Jake turned and looked over his shoulder, wondering if anyone would notice if he got into the car with Moses. If he ended up dead in a ditch somewhere, there would at least be enough witnesses to describe the car, maybe even a glimpse of Moses's crazy hair. But when Jake scanned the skaters behind him and realized no one was even remotely paying attention to anything or anyone outside the park, all hope of being rescued was instantly lost.

His mind raced to find another way out. Perhaps he

could outrun them. He knew every nook, cranny, and backstreet in Weyport. He would chance that they didn't know where he lived so he could easily jump the fence and cut through the woodland. But if he failed, and they did know or even saw where he was heading, he'd be putting his entire family at risk. And that he couldn't let happen.

His mind conjured up images of Moses and his men barging into his house, scaring his mother and Teddy who were home alone during the day. A chill ran down his spine and he pushed the thoughts aside. There was only one way to deal with this.

Abandoning the idea of running away like a coward, he decided that it was better to pluck up the courage and face Moses like a man instead. After all, he'd heard his mother teach to always face the enemy head-on. Besides, he had learned more than a few wrestling moves over the years that could very well help him should it come to that.

Content with his decision, Jake turned and started walking toward the black car. But as he closed in on it, Sheriff Reid's white SUV pulled up in the parking bay to the left of him.

Jake stopped, his eyes anxiously darting between Moses and the new town sheriff. If he now got into the car with Moses, Sheriff Reid was bound to ask questions, if he made it out alive. And if he spoke to the sheriff, Moses would think he was a snitch. Neither option would play out in his favor no matter which way he played it.

Frozen to the spot, his heart pounding in his chest, Jake searched for answers in Moses's eyes. What greeted him instead were chilling signs of warning to stay back and walk away. So he did.

But when Sheriff Reid flashed Jake a suspicious look before his gaze drifted to the beefy man who was hastily getting into the black car, Jake knew the sheriff had caught on that something strange was going on.

Nerves churned as Jake watched the sheriff exit his vehicle and walk toward the black car. But before he was able to reach it, Moses had already disappeared behind his tinted window as they hastily backed out of the parking and drove off.

Jake didn't hang about and he spun around, desperate to avoid being questioned by the sheriff.

But there was no escaping him.

"Hey, Jacob, wait up!" Angus yelled after him.

Jake kept walking. Hoping, praying the sheriff would give up his pursuit.

Angus stepped up his pace and called out to Jacob again, lightly jogging the last few strides to close the gap between them. When he reached Jacob, he pulled back on his shoulder, turning the teen around to face him.

"Jacob, wait up, son. Did you not hear me calling you?"

Unable to escape the sheriff's searching eyes, Jake replied with feigned enthusiasm.

"I did, Sheriff, but I'm late for dinner. Sorry, I have to go."

He tried turning away to leave, or hide his guilt, but Angus gently grabbed his arm.

"Who were those guys back there, Jacob?" Angus asked, his gaze fixed on Jacob's whose eyes were wide as he looked up at Angus. And for the smallest of moments, Angus was certain he had seen traces of fear behind them. But then, as quickly as the teenager hinted at the truth, his eyes shut away his emotions.

Jake didn't answer. Less is more, he thought.

"I know I interrupted something back there, Jacob. Talk to me. I give you my word it will stay between us." Angus tried again, his voice now more gentle.

Jacob shrugged his shoulders. "I don't know what you're talking about, Sheriff. I have to go home now."

But in the pit of Angus's stomach, he sensed Jacob knew precisely what he was talking about. Eight years in the Clark County Sheriff's Office had taught him to recognize trouble when he saw it. But he also knew if he pushed too hard it might scare Jacob away for good.

"It's going to be dark soon. Come, I'll take you home. I'm going that way anyway."

The doubtful look on Jacob's face told Angus the boy needed more reassurance so he added, "I promise I won't ask you any more questions, okay? Not unless you choose to tell me about it yourself. I just need you to know that

I'm here for you if ever you find yourself in a sticky situation." Angus knew to choose his words carefully.

Jake scanned the perimeter of the skate park for any signs that Moses might be lingering or watching him. But when he couldn't see his men or the black vehicle anywhere, he decided to take the sheriff up on his offer, just in case Moses came back to finish what he came there to do.

Jake nodded in agreement and Angus curled his arm around Jake's shoulders and ushered him toward his car.

As agreed, Angus didn't ask Jacob anything else about the incident. Instead, he made small talk about the fish he had in his aquarium back home in Las Vegas. Although the topic seemed to somewhat relax Jacob, he kept to himself for most of the short drive to his home.

It took a generous amount of self-control for Angus not to push Jake for answers. But over the years, he had worked with a fair number of teenagers during his career and knew that gaining their trust was paramount to achieving a breakthrough. And although this wasn't a case, he'd have to approach it the same way.

CHAPTER TWELVE

Angus circled the neighborhood a few more times after he safely dropped Jacob at his house and watched him go inside. When, after several hours, there wasn't any sign of the black car, he drove past the skate park. A thick fog had settled over the park like a hazy protective blanket, wrapping over the ramps as if it too was sensing something was amiss.

Parked up next to the park, Angus rolled down his window and allowed the cold night air to caress his face while he scanned the dark corners between the skating ramps. A forbidding sense of danger hung thick in the air and settled on the back of his neck as an uncontrollable quiver tingled down his spine. Something wasn't quite right. He could feel it, with every fiber of his being. He prayed that he was wrong. That God would keep Jacob safe. That God would spare him another tragedy.

Emotions suddenly overwhelmed his senses. As if something duty-bound propelled him to protect Jacob and his family. He'd only met the boy and his family once, but there was something that drew him to want to spend more time with them. Perhaps it was a longing for what could have been. A yearning for what he once had and then lost. Perhaps it was hope that he'd have it again someday. Lunching with the Foleys had scratched at old wounds but it had also strangely offered healing. Hope. If things hadn't turned out the way they did, if only he hadn't put his career first, he might have had a family of his own. Had what they had. He counted the dates in his head. His son would have been ten years old by now, the age most kids started skateboarding. Sadness teased at his memories. It felt like a lifetime ago. He recalled the broken-heartedness in his ex-wife's face after they had lost their unborn baby boy. The guilt he felt for not being there when they needed him most. He was pulling an all-nighter in the office, working a case he couldn't even remember right now. He should have been home, with her and their baby. Perhaps if he were there, where he was supposed to be, keeping his wife and baby safe, he could have prevented it. If only he had gotten her to the hospital sooner she might not have gone into early labor, and they'd have had their son and still been together. Just like the Foleys.

A lonely tear trickled down his cheek and he wiped it with the back of his hand. It didn't matter anymore. It was in the past. He couldn't change it even if he wanted to. It was what had brought him to his knees and how he found Jesus—forgiveness. Even though it was closure he sought most.

He pulled a deep breath of crisp air into his lungs, forced his mind back to the present then drove the short distance back to his room at the Old Mill.

Despite the fact that there was no sign of the ominous black vehicle, Angus was restless until deep into the night. He had drifted in and out of sleep, his heart and mind too troubled to be at peace. He had taken note of the beefy guy who stood staring at Jacob and the black tinted windows on the car that was parked next to him. Guys like that usually worked for someone else. And if experience told him nothing else, it was that narcotics were somehow involved. He knew the signs. His instincts told him Jacob could be in trouble and, as the town sheriff, it was up to him to make sure the boy was safe. This time he'd be there before something bad happened.

Whoever was hiding inside that black car was now meddling in his business. Weyport was now his to protect, a duty he didn't take lightly. And if it took him the rest of his life, he would rid this town of the seedy criminals Pete Hutchinson had selfishly sanctioned all these years. One criminal at a time.

Thoughts swirled inside his head as Angus stared at his clock radio. He had gotten used to waking up at four a.m. and even liked it. But he'd not once been awake before the alarm went off. Though he was physically exhausted, his mind was now wide-awake, and with twenty minutes on the clock to spare, he decided he'd head to his office earlier than usual. He was of no use lying around in bed, watching time pass him by. The sooner he got to work the sooner he could access the database and hopefully, track down whoever owned the black vehicle. He'd start there.

As had become routine by now, Angus took the long way into the office, driving through the neighborhood and past Mrs. Richardson's house, which was still dark and quiet. He had skipped dinner the night before and suddenly he craved more of her granola cookies, which he had already finished. A smile broke on his face when from her dark living room, the curtains moved ever so slightly. She must already be up, watching to see if he delivered on his promise. Or perhaps, like him, she sensed danger and stood guard over her neighborhood.

The thought spurred Angus on even more. He owed it to her, the Foleys, and the whole of Weyport to make sure they were all safe.

He stepped on the gas, in sudden haste to get behind his desk. He had busied himself with a few minor open cases that were left unresolved when Pete left. But as he pulled his chair closer to his desk, he pushed the small stack of folders to one side and switched on his computer.

It was only once Tammy spoke behind him that he suddenly realized he'd been so consumed by his search for the black vehicle that he hadn't even realized the time it took.

"Sheriff, have you been here all night?" Tammy's chipper voice startled him and he nearly spilled the last bit of his cold mug of coffee across his desk.

"Oops! Sorry, Sheriff, didn't mean to startle you." She flashed a smile and cleared the cold coffee away. "I'll take that. Looks like you need a fresh one," Tammy added.

"That's all right, thank you. I'm going to pop over to the diner and grab something to eat. I could do with clearing my head."

"What's got you so busy that you are at it so hard, Sheriff?" She leaned closer to the computer screen where rows of black vehicles spread across the screen.

"Just trying to locate a suspicious vehicle I spotted lurking at the skate park yesterday."

"Seems like you're struggling," she commented.

Angus scratched the back of his head as he leaned back in his office chair, bending the backrest into a reclining position.

"I am. I didn't think there were so many of these registered in the county."

"You didn't get a partial on the registration?"

"Nope. Not even a bumper sticker."

"So, if I may ask, Sheriff, what was so suspicious about this vehicle?"

Angus stood up and grabbed his jacket off the back of his chair, his mind racing to rationalize an answer.

"Truthfully, nothing in particular. It's just a gut feeling." He slipped the jacket on and then added, "I'll see you in a bit. I'll be at the diner down the street if you need me."

He locked his computer and pulled his door closed behind them before he made his way to the diner. When he stepped inside, the smell of bacon and fresh coffee triggered his senses as hunger pangs overtook him. By now, he had frequented the diner, relying on their wholesome food at least once a day.

"The usual, Sheriff?" Monica, one of the servers asked as he slipped into his now usual booth.

"Yes, please, extra bacon today though."

"Coming right up, Sheriff." She poured his coffee before placing a receipt on a nearby table in passing.

The middle-aged couple at the table had been looking at Angus, doubt written all over their faces as they whispered to each other. Angus tipped his head in greeting but they ignored him. Great, he thought. Two more townsfolk who didn't yet trust him.

With his thoughts his own, he let them be. He had a lot to prove to this town and a mountain to climb while doing it.

CHAPTER THIRTEEN

Angus was halfway through his breakfast when his mobile phone rang. It was Tammy. He answered it quickly, his mouth still full from his last bite of food.

"Sorry to interrupt, Sheriff," Tammy blurted out. "We have a case that requires your urgent attention. A missing teen."

The food lodged in the back of Angus's throat as his thoughts immediately drifted to Jacob. Tammy's announcement had left him cold; fear and anger simultaneously flooding his veins.

"I'm on my way," he announced, forcing the food down with two mouthfuls of coffee.

Leaving a few bills and a generous tip behind on the table, he stormed out of the diner and made his way to the office.

When he burst through the front doors of his office,

expecting to see Joe, Jacob's father, Tammy was trying to pacify a man who looked like life had gotten the better of him. Relief washed over him as he realized that this had to be the alleged missing teen's father.

Tammy's eyes shot a distressed look his way. It was clear she couldn't handle the man's panicked ramblings.

Rushing to her aid, Angus laid one hand on the anguished father's shoulder.

"Why don't we step into my office, sir?" he said.

When the man spun around, a strong odor of liquor hit Angus's nostrils and he flinched.

"Let's get you a fresh cup of strong coffee while we're at it, shall we?" Motioning toward Tammy to rush the coffee, Angus sent a rapid double lift of his eyebrows toward her. Right away, she fled toward the coffee pot.

"Take a seat, Mr. ..." Angus hinted for the man's name as he ushered him into a chair opposite him at his desk.

"McGee, Raymond McGee but everyone just calls me Ray."

When the man spoke, Angus noticed he was missing several teeth; the rest of what was left were badly decayed.

"Good to meet you, Ray. I'm Sheriff Angus Reid. Why don't you start at the beginning and tell me what brought you here today."

Ray nodded, his eyes scanning Angus's face.

"It's okay, Ray. I know I'm new here and we don't know each other but I assure you, I am well equipped to handle whatever you throw at me. Who do you think is missing?"

The man's nicotine-stained hands wrapped over the wooden armrests of his chair, his fingernails yellow and dirty. He hovered there for a few seconds as if he was still unsure if he could trust Angus.

Angus didn't push him for fear of driving the man away. So he waited and allowed Ray to run his assessment of him. Just then, Tammy entered with Ray's coffee and placed it down in front of him.

"Drink up, Ray. The sheriff's going to need you sober if he's to find Aaron." When Ray hesitated to take his coffee, his eyes still darting between Tammy and Angus, she added, "You can trust him, Ray. He's the new sheriff now so the way I see it, he's all you got right now." She disguised a subtle smile directed at Angus before she turned and left them alone.

Tammy's good word seemed to have done the trick and Ray settled into his chair and then noisily gulped down the coffee that was so strong it would knock over a bull. When he was done, he put the Styrofoam cup back on the desk and wiped his mouth on his sleeve.

"It's my son, Aaron. He didn't come home yesterday. I thought he was just running late with work but when he wasn't home today either I knew something must be wrong. It's not like him. No matter what, he's always home to wake me up and take me to work."

Angus furrowed his brow.

"You work nightshifts then?"

Ray pulled his face in annoyance.

"Nightshift? No. Are you not paying attention, Sheriff?"

"I am but I thought you said he's always home to wake you up for work. I just assumed you meant you worked at night if he was late coming from work."

A strange look flashed across Ray's face before he spoke again, his words now stuttered.

"I work at the boatyard. He goes to Weyport High. He always wakes me up and takes me to work."

"Except he didn't yesterday morning nor today," Angus verified.

Ray nodded.

"I see. How old is your son, Ray?"

"Nineteen."

Angus tilted his head in question.

"He's not the brightest kid in school, Sheriff, but he's doing his best. Since his mother left us and took everything we owned with her, left us high and dry when he was only thirteen, he's done his part in keeping a roof over our heads," Ray defended, his voice irate.

"I'm not judging, Ray. I just needed some clarification. You said he helps with money. What does he do?"

Ray didn't answer immediately.

"This and that, odd jobs wherever he can."

"Where is he working at the moment"

Ray fidgeted in his chair.

"I don't know," he lied.

Angus paused to study Ray's face. The man was hiding something, he could tell but he decided to shift gears for the moment.

"I take it you contacted the school?"

Ray nodded. "He never went in yesterday and he's not gone in today either."

Angus glanced at the clock on the wall.

"It's still early, though, Ray. Perhaps he's just late."

Ray stood up, his hands now flat on the desk as he faced Angus.

"You said you'd help me, Sheriff! But all you've done is ask a million questions and pass judgment. My boy is missing. Why aren't you trying to find him? If Sheriff Pete were here he would have been out there looking for my boy already!"

Every cell in Angus's body wanted to shout out just how corrupt his beloved Sheriff Pete was but he held back his annoyance. For all he knew Raymond McGee was one of the townsfolk Pete conveniently turned a blind eye for.

"I'm sorry, Ray. I'm just trying to cover all the angles. Please, sit down. When did you last see him?"

It took another moment or two before Ray sank back down in his chair and answered the question.

"I briefly saw him the night before last, when I got home from work."

"I'm listening."

"He had gone to school and everything was fine.

When I got home, we grilled a couple of burgers and had a few beers together. That was it."

"Except he wasn't there when you woke up yesterday morning."

"Exactly." Nerves clung to Ray's face as he shuffled in his chair.

"What else?" Angus prodded, still sensing Ray was holding back on him.

"Well, he did get a call. I don't know who from but he left in quite a bit of a hurry afterward."

"Did he say where he was going?"

"No, but then he never does."

"So, he does this often, leaves after he gets a call?"

Ray nodded.

Angus jotted down a few notes on his desk pad.

"I'm going to need his cell number, please, Ray."

"I don't have it, at least not here. I don't have a mobile. I've never quite gotten the hang of those things."

"You have it at home then?"

"Yes, it's on the refrigerator, just in case there's an emergency. I usually call him from the phone booth near our house. But it's of no use anyway, Sheriff. I already called it before I came here. It's not even ringing."

Angus got to his feet and snatched his car keys from his desk drawer.

"I'll need it in any event, Ray. I can follow you home if you don't mind?"

"I don't drive, Sheriff. I grabbed a ride in with Bill. He owns one of the boats I'm working on down at the yard."

"Then I'll give you a ride back home and get that number from you while I'm there. Sound good?"

Ray agreed and jumped to his feet, now eager to help however he could.

CHAPTER FOURTEEN

The McGees lived at the edge of Weyport in a trailer park about a mile outside of town. As they drove in and got a few curious stares from residents in passing, Ray leaned his head out of the window and yelled, "What ya looking at, you bunch of busybodies? Ain't nothing here for you to see!"

His aggressive reaction was reciprocated by obscene spats and gestures, which left him mumbling words of disdain under his breath.

"You don't get on with your neighbors much, do you, Ray?" Angus commented.

"They're nothing but meddlers, sitting around gossiping all day. They stay out of our way and we stay out of theirs. That's how I like it. Turn up here," he added as he pointed one dirty fingernail toward a lonely trailer on the far end of the park.

Set on a small hill that overlooked the rest of the park, the beige and chocolate brown trailer had seen better days, its roof was rusted in places and the front awning torn as if a flight of seagulls had dived through it. A wire fence ran the perimeter, carving out a substantial piece of ground around the trailer. Scattered throughout were a few old tires, some of which were stacked atop each other like little towers. In front of the trailer, a tatty burgundy pleather couch was pushed up against the trailer, and next to it was a shiny gas barbecue.

"It's not much but it's home," Ray excused when he saw the way Angus took it all in.

"Looks pretty tranquil to me, Ray. I've been living out of a small room at the Old Mill for the past few months. I'd love to have a nice piece of land like this. Not to mention having me one of those outdoor grills."

Angus was hinting for information on how the McGees could afford such an expensive griller.

"Yeah, we like it. It was even better before all of them busybodies pushed their way in," Ray said, omitting any comment on the barbecue.

Instead, Ray yanked open the trailer door and Angus followed him inside. Surprisingly, the place was as neat as a pin with not a dirty dish or empty beer can in sight.

"We like it clean and tidy," Ray said, pride written all over his face. "Aaron says a clean space is a clean mind. He does most of the chores around here though. He's a good boy."

Ray stepped up to the refrigerator and pulled a piece of paper from under a magnet that looked like a casino chip, the local casino's logo printed in the center.

He handed the paper with a single mobile number on to Angus then snatched it back. "Wait, it's my only copy. Let me write it down for you, Sheriff."

"I'll just jot it down in my pocketbook, Ray, thanks," Angus said as he pulled the book and pen from his breast pocket and started copying the number.

"Do you play?" Angus asked, briefly pointing the back of his pen at the black and red casino magnet.

"Mostly weekends, yes. It beats sitting around here listening to the cackling of that bunch down there. How about you, Sheriff? You look like a poker man to me."

Angus stifled a giggle. "I'm afraid I'm not much of a gambling man, Ray. Can you show me where Aaron sleeps?" he asked, changing the conversation back to matters at hand.

"Yeah, yeah, this way," Ray said as he led Angus to the other end of the trailer and opened one of the doors.

Once more Angus was met with a room that was both clean and tidy. The bright red bed cover was perfectly made and not a piece of dirty laundry lay anywhere.

"You weren't joking, were you? Your boy certainly likes a tidy room. Most teenagers I've met are messy. You've raised him well, Ray."

"He takes after his mother." Ray looked off into the

distance before he snapped back to the present. "Anyway, I told you, he's not here."

"Sorry to ask, Ray, but I have to cover all possibilities. Does he have any contact with his mother?"

Ray scoffed, anger suddenly flooding his eyes.

"No. Absolutely not. He wants nothing to do with her. Frankly, I don't want to either. She's never setting foot near us again."

"I understand. Is there anything else you can tell me, Ray? Anything at all. Who his friends are, where he likes to hang out, that type of thing."

Ray shook his head.

"He takes the bus to school and back and he's never brought anyone home, not once. I guess he just likes to hide all this and pretend we live in one of those rich neighborhoods up the coast." Ray turned away and squeezed in behind the table of the eating corner, rubbing his palms over his face before he spoke again. "He's never stayed away, Sheriff. Even when we've had one of those father-son fights. We've always sorted it out. Please, Sheriff. You have to find my son. He's all I have in this world. I might not be the world's best dad and yes, there have been times when I looked too deep down the bottle and the liquor made me act like an idiot but we have always been a family. We've always been there for each other, taken care of one another just like a father and son are supposed to do, you know?"

Angus didn't know.

"I'll do everything I can to find him, Ray. I give you my word. In the meantime, I suggest you stay here in case he comes home. If he does, or you recall anything that might help us find him, you call me directly, okay?" Angus handed him a business card then turned and left.

The drive back had Angus restless. He'd handled many missing persons' cases over the years, but it was hardest when a minor was involved. Sometimes it would be a simple case of a runaway teen, but this one somehow felt different. He'd seen Aaron's room, seen the circumstances they lived in, and had looked deep into Ray's eyes. There was nothing there that gave him reason to believe the boy had run away from home. No signs of any struggle. No evidence of foul play. He knew the signs.

But then he also knew that most people had at least one secret; teens and young adults had more than a few. Ray was holding back, that much he had already figured out. What that was, time would tell.

He turned his car's nose toward the school. He'd start there. If Aaron had any friends, he'd find them there.

CHAPTER FIFTEEN

J ake's leg nervously bounced up and down beneath his desk. His eyes were pinned to the clock on the wall behind his history teacher. Generally, he'd be soaking in every word his teacher spoke, but these past two days Jake couldn't maintain his focus in any of his classes.

After Aaron didn't turn up as agreed in the skate park, he'd kept a low profile, asking his mother to take him to school and back instead of taking the bus. Although he remained convinced that Moses didn't know where he lived, he didn't want to take any chances. He had dialed Aaron's number several times since then but never got any answer. Not even a reply to any of the SMS messages he'd sent. And when Aaron didn't show up for school yesterday, he was convinced something terrible had happened.

In a few days, there would be another meeting at the houseboat and Moses would be expecting his money.

Money Jake didn't have. Without Aaron's help, there was no way he could settle what he owed. And no way he could continue his side hustle. It had turned into a mess. One he had no idea how to clean up.

When the bell finally rang, Jake shot out of his chair and made a beeline for the door. It was first break and he had thought of taking one more shot at finding Aaron in the event he might have turned up late for school. He hurried through the hallways, bumping into several of the kids along the way until he reached their usual meet-up spot behind the bleachers. Two of his classmates were already there and they had just lit a cigarette. But there was no sign of Aaron.

"Hey, guys, have you seen Aaron today?" Jake asked, to which both replied that he hadn't come to school again.

"Okay, thanks. If you see him or talk to him, tell him I really need to speak to him. It's urgent, okay?"

"Does this have something to do with why the new sheriff was here looking for him?" one boy asked.

His question left Jake cold.

"Sheriff Reid was here, at school?"

"Yeah, man, we owe him big time for letting us all off the hook with our chemistry test. I would have for sure flunked it, dude!" They chuckled between themselves.

But nothing they had just told him brought Jake any joy. He trailed off to a quiet corner of the school where he slumped down on the ground, leaning against one of the walls. If something bad had happened to Aaron, Sheriff

Reid would, for certain, put two and two together. Everyone on the school bus had seen them sitting together of late. The sheriff was way too smart not to figure it out, especially after he nearly caught him meeting up with Moses in the skate park the other day. Jake was in agony. Backed into a corner, with no way out. He was a terrible liar and if questioned about Aaron, his mother would be the first to tell he was lying. He contemplated trusting her by telling her everything. What if Aaron was still alive, perhaps even in the bear pit Moses warned about? If there was a chance he could help him, he should.

He dropped his face onto his knees and crossed his arms over his head. Tears sat shallow behind his eyes, his heart now heavy with regret. If Aaron died because of him, he would never be able to forgive himself. Nor would God who he had once promised his heart to.

When at the end of the day, Jake's mother picked him up from school he could barely look her way and quietly sat staring out the window instead. He had caught her glancing at him sideways a few times but thankfully escaped her usual probing questions about school when she got stuck talking on her phone to one of the church members for most of the way. When they pulled up to their house, Sheriff Reid's car was parked in the driveway.

"Oh, how nice of him to drop by," MJ said as they parked up.

Jake didn't say a word. He already knew why he was there.

MJ was out of the car and on the porch in no time, eager to extend her hospitality to their town sheriff.

"Mom, wait," Jake said as she was about to open the front door. "I need to tell you something."

"Sure, my boy, but can it maybe wait until later? We don't want to be rude and keep Sheriff Angus waiting." She squeezed his arm and then turned to open the door.

Jake wanted to stop her, tell her what he had been up to, why the sheriff was there. But the brief surge of courage he had mustered mere moments ago was no longer there. In its place, was nothing but regret and fear.

MJ burst through the door in her usual cheerful manner.

"Hello, Sheriff? What a pleasant surprise?" she said as she set down a bag of shopping in the kitchen where Angus and Joe sat at the small table in the center.

Jake watched from the doorway, his stepfather's eyes suddenly upon him.

"He's here on official business, MJ. I think you had better sit down for this one."

Jake made for his room.

"Not so fast, Jacob. Sheriff Reid needs to speak to you," Joe yelled after him.

MJ's head spun around to search her husband's face for answers.

"I'm confused. What's going on? Why do you want to speak to my son, Sheriff?" MJ's voice was tinged with caution as she pulled Jake into a chair beside her, her arm protectively draped around the back.

"I just need to ask him a couple of questions about a boy named Aaron McGee," Angus said, his eyes studying Jake's reaction.

"We don't know anyone with that name, Sheriff. And I know all Jacob's friends from as far back as kindergarten." MJ's guard was up.

"With respect, MJ, I think Jacob knows whom I'm talking about," Angus replied, his eyes still on Jake.

"Jacob, who's he talking about? Do you know someone by that name?" MJ said again, unable to let her protective guard down.

"Perhaps we should let Angus do the talking, MJ," Joe interrupted, patting his hand on her arm.

She pulled her arm away, annoyed at her husband's patronizing gesture.

"I think I have every right to know why he's here asking my son all sorts of questions about a man we don't know, Joe." MJ spat back before she turned to face Angus. "Tell me what all this is about right now, Sheriff. As his mother, I demand you tell me." MJ's voice was stern, her eyes filled with defense for her son.

"The boy's gone missing, MJ, and I have reason to believe Jacob might know something that could help us find him."

Angus waited for Jake to talk, his gaze fixed on Jacob's concerned expression.

Jacob stalled, frozen in place like a deer caught in headlights.

Panic gripped at his throat and settled in his chest before it forced its way into his legs and ejected him off his chair.

CHAPTER SIXTEEN

Unable to control the reaction that had taken over his body Jake ran, out the front door and down the street toward the woodland path. Every sensation inside his cells told him to flee. As fast and as far away from the guilt and shame he had brought over his family as his legs would carry him. Panic made way for fear and eventually sadness as he ran between the trees, his heart pulsing in his constricted throat. He couldn't stop, didn't stop. Not even once did he look back to see if Sheriff Reid was chasing after him. All he could do was run.

Hardly registering his surroundings, Jake cut through the forest and followed the dense tree line to where it eventually stopped at the edge of town before it stretched out along the coastal road. Exhaustion grabbed at his stringy body but he kept going. Through the dense trees and over the soft leafy ground, nearly twisting his ankles a few times, but he kept moving. Tears ran freely down his cheeks, his heart squeezing tight inside his chest. But he couldn't stop. It had all gotten too much for him. Fear for what happened to Aaron. Fear over what would happen to him. Fear of judgment once everyone knew what he had been doing.

When his mind finally caught up to his body, or his body at long last gave in, he was at the edge of the forest where the trees met the old coastal road. He stopped, catching his breath next to a big fir tree, his hand pinching at the sharp pain in his side as he stopped to take in his surroundings for the first time.

Oblivious to where his legs had carried him, unable to take hold of his shame, he found himself staring at the sandy road that led down to the clearing and eventually the houseboat.

As his breath returned to normal and panic soon settled to a faint flutter in his stomach, Jake's mind kicked into action. Aaron was missing. That's why he couldn't get hold of him. That's why he never showed up at the skate park.

From where he stood on a slight mound overlooking the road at the edge of the woods, he could see all the way to where the clearing stretched out between the sand dunes across the road in front of him. Staying hidden between the trees, he stood there for a while, carefully scouting the makeshift parking for signs of Aaron's car. But when he didn't see it, his mind trailed to the chance encounter with Moses at the skate park. Moses had somehow tracked him down even though he'd never seen his face. Perhaps he had done the same with Aaron.

Perhaps Aaron wasn't so lucky to escape him.

Dread suddenly pushed into his throat. Aaron had stepped in to help him, to cover for him, to save his skin. And now Moses had taken him instead.

He couldn't let that happen. He couldn't let Aaron take the fall for his mistake. It wasn't right. That much he knew.

He would face his enemy head-on, and own up to what he had done. No matter the consequences.

MJ PACED the floor in her kitchen, one hand clutching the strand of pearls around her neck. Behind her, Joe sat at the table building a thousand-piece puzzle with Teddy.

Outside it had gone dark already, the neighborhood blissfully unaware of the drama that was unfolding around them.

She looked up at the kitchen clock. It had just gone eight thirty in the evening and Jacob hadn't returned yet. Nor had they heard anything back from Angus.

"It's been hours, Joe. Why haven't we heard anything yet?" MJ eventually said, her voice drenched with angst.

Joe glanced at the clock and popped another piece into the puzzle.

"It's still early. For all we know he's at the skate park. Let's wait until his curfew. If he's not back by nine, I'll call Angus for an update."

MJ came to stand next to one of the chairs, her hands white as they wrapped around the backrest.

"Did you see his face, Joe? He was scared witless. I've never seen him like that."

"The boy is seventeen, MJ. He's bound to have gotten himself into some kind of trouble by now. We all do at his age." Joe said before he playfully rubbed at the back of Teddy's head praising him for finding a tricky piece of the puzzle.

"And you don't think we should be concerned at all, Joe? Jacob isn't like most teens. He's never been in any kind of trouble, especially not with the law."

"You're assuming he's in trouble, MJ. Sheriff Angus only wanted to ask him about the missing boy. He probably just ran a bit scared. I think you should stay calm and not get ahead of yourself now. He'll be back. And if I know Jacob, it will be when hunger prompts it. You'll see, he'll walk through that door any time now." Joe turned his attention to Teddy. "In the meantime, young man, let's get you ready for bed. We'll carry on with the puzzle tomorrow after school, okay?"

Teddy pushed another puzzle piece into the picture and flattened it with his palm.

"Heroes need ice cream," he said, repeating it a few times.

Joe laughed, curiosity in his eyes as he looked at Teddy.

"So you've been saying now for a while, my boy. Is it from one of those programs you've been watching, huh?"

"Jacob says heroes get stronger when they eat ice cream. I want ice cream. The one under my bed," Teddy continued, inviting a curious head tilt from his mother.

"Okay, time to brush your teeth and scoot off to bed. It's too late for ice cream now," she said.

"But heroes need ice cream. Jacob says, Jacob says." Teddy repeated with frustration.

"Oh, Jacob says, does he? Well, he should know better, Teddy." MJ reached for the ice cream from the fridge drawer. "One scoop, okay? We don't want you getting a tummy ache."

"Not that one. I want the one from my room, under my bed. That one has sprinkles." Teddy was already off his chair and on the way to his room, both his mother and Joe in tow.

They watched as Teddy knelt down and reached under his bed to retrieve a small cooler. Popping it on top of his bed he flipped the lid open, revealing four store-bought mini ice cream pots from which he chose one before throwing the rest back into the cooler.

"I guess he wasn't kidding around," Joe said, looking at MJ's stunned face.

"Teddy, where did you get those?" MJ asked from where she now sat next to him on the edge of the bed.

"Heroes have secrets. Jacob says," Teddy replied.

"Are you the hero, Teddy? Do you have a secret?"

Teddy didn't reply, his mouth now covered in choco-late mint ice cream.

Just then, the phone rang in the kitchen.

Abandoning the inquiry, MJ rushed to go answer, Joe in her wake.

"Hello, this is MJ."

"MJ, it's Angus. I'm just ringing to find out if Jacob's found his way home yet."

Distress flashed across MJ's face.

"You haven't found him? He's not here, Angus. I thought you said you had an idea where he was." MJ was clutching her pearls again.

"Yeah, unfortunately, that turned up empty. I had hoped he was hanging out at the skate park. It's where I spotted him the other day."

MJ's heart was in her stomach, her eyes now wide with concern as she looked to Joe for support.

"We have to find him, Angus. I have a terrible feeling about this," MJ spoke into the receiver, her fingers now twisting around the phone cord.

"It might be a bit too early for concern, MJ. The boy probably just ran scared and needed some timeout," Angus said.

"That's what Joe's saying too but I'm not so sure. This isn't like him. Jacob doesn't just run off like that. Some-thing is wrong, Angus. I can feel it."

Angus went briefly quiet then spoke again.

"Fine, I'll take another drive by the skate park and crisscross through town to see if I can find him. In the meantime, perhaps you want to call up his friends, anyone you think he might have gone to hang out with. Stay home and stay close to the phone. I'll keep in touch."

Shocked into silence MJ nodded as Angus ended the call.

CHAPTER SEVENTEEN

MJ paced the dark corners of her living room. Stopping briefly, she pulled back the drapes and looked out into the dark street for what seemed like the thousandth time. When it once again yielded nothing, she went into the kitchen to make another cup of lavender-infused tea. She'd already had two and it did little to nothing to settle the uneasy feeling that lingered inside her gut. It had been hours since Jacob ran out of the house and he'd still not returned home. She had called all his friends in the hopes that he had gone to one of them but to no avail. No one had seen or heard from him. Even Angus rang earlier to say his search throughout the neighborhood had also turned up empty. It was all he could do since he had no concrete grounds for filing an official missing person's report. All they could do now was hope and pray that he'd turn up.

Feeling utterly helpless and with a fresh cup of tea now in hand, she returned to the living room, setting the cup down on the coffee table before she made her way back to the window. Her eyes darted up and down the poorly lit street, pausing between the tall fir trees in the woodland opposite the road. Somewhere out there, in the cold dark night, her beloved son was vulnerable and alone, probably also afraid. A sudden thought crossed her mind. Was he with someone? Perhaps the Aaron boy Angus had said went missing a few days before. Perhaps Jacob did know who and where he was.

Fear tightened her throat. But what if the opposite had happened? What if Jacob had gone missing too? Just like Aaron. What if there was a deranged man out there snatching up young, defenseless teenagers? A serial killer even. What if her Jacob was dealt the same fate as the other boy? For all she knew, her son was in trouble, lying somewhere helpless and barely alive.

A million thoughts suddenly rushed through her mind all at once and fear instantly overwhelmed her senses. Unable to drown them out she fell back against the wall behind the curtain and shut her eyes. Desperate she turned her thoughts to God. Not my boy, please, Lord, not my beautiful baby boy, she prayed a silent prayer. Spare me that pain, Lord Jesus. I won't survive losing my boy. I won't survive it!

But the more she pleaded with God, the harder it got to drown out the fear.

Memories of Jacob as a baby flooded her mind as the tears rolled down her already wet cheeks. He was so young when his father died and it had been just the two of them for a while before she met Joe and became a stepmother to Teddy. Jacob was everything to her. Her life. The very beat of her heart. She couldn't exist without him. Wouldn't know how.

Unable to bear the thought of losing her only son, she sank into one of the sofa seats and buried her face in her hands, praying God would spare her son. Praying that God would be with him. Praying that He would bring him home safely.

Tears drenched her hands and she reached for the Kleenex in the pocket of her robe. But as was so typical of Mary-Jean Foley, her mind kicked into defense mode. No. She fought off the negativity in her mind, her feet suddenly ejecting her body upright. He's not dead. Jacob is fine. He was strong, like her, a fighter. It's in his genes and he's the smartest boy she'd ever known. Whatever his reasons were for fleeing the house earlier she was certain it was necessary. She straightened her robe and wiped her tears before she reached for her cup of tea, resilience now guarding her heart.

But less than five minutes on, after she drained the tea in one go, doubt found its way back into her mind and she started pacing the room once more.

She glanced at the time on her small gold wristwatch and twisted the narrow, worn leather strap into place around her wrist. It was nearly two thirty in the morning and the uneasy feeling deep inside her stomach remained in place. She couldn't sit around and wait, she thought. She'd never been dealt the hand of patience. She was a doer. A woman who against any odds would fight her way through adversity. It was the very reason she took on so much at church; why she was known to be dependable in all circumstances. She had never been one to idly sit around and wait for things to happen. And she wasn't going to start now.

Resolute on finding her son herself, she spun around and set off to the bedroom. Joe's gentle snores purred into her ears as she walked past their bed to her closet. Pulling her jeans and a sweater on, she found herself looking back at her husband. How was it that he could sleep without a worry in the world when their son was out there somewhere? And as quickly as the question came to her, so did its answer. Because in truth, Joe wasn't Jacob's father. Not related by blood anyway. Sure, he had taken on the responsibility when they got married, and he'd been good at it in the ordinary fatherly things, but Joe and Jacob's relationship was just that, ordinary. Almost mechanical. Joe could never share the bond she had with Jacob.

Annoyance tugged at her insides but she let it go. Moments later she was at the front door.

"Where are you going?" Joe's voice suddenly sounded behind her.

Startled she dropped the car keys onto the floor.

"Joe! You nearly gave me a stroke." She bent to pick the keys up. "I can't just sit around and do nothing, Joe. I'm going to go look for my son."

"Now? It's the middle of the night. I think you're over-reacting, MJ. Teens do this type of thing all the time. He's probably with one of his friends."

"Jacob isn't like other teens, Joe. If you were closer to him you'd know that."

Annoyance still bitter in the back of her throat, she wrapped her scarf around her neck; far too tight, she tugged at it to loosen the bit that was now choking her. When she looked up at Joe who had gone quiet, his eyes told her the words she so callously slung at him moments before had cut deep into his soul.

Regret settled in the back of her mind. He was a good man, always had been. He didn't deserve her scorn.

"I'm sorry," she mumbled as she straightened her hair. "I'm just really worried about him, Joe. This isn't like him and I can't shake this feeling that something is terribly wrong."

Joe pulled her closer. To forgive easily was one of his superpowers.

"I know. I am too. But going out there now in the dark to look for him is foolish. Where would you even look that Angus hadn't searched already? Let's wait until morning, and see if he turns up for school. If not, I'll call Angus myself to file that report. I don't think you should jump to any conclusions, MJ. He's a kid. Kids run away from reality all the time. It's the new normal these days to hide your feelings from the world. He probably just needs a bit of alone time."

MJ pushed herself away from Joe, tears now running down her cheeks once more.

"You don't understand, Joe. He's my son. My *son!*"

Her heart pushed to a lump in her throat but she forced it down as she slipped on her coat.

"I'm going out there to find my son and bring him home, Joe, and there's nothing you can do to stop me. God forbid he's lying half dead in a ditch somewhere and I could have helped him. I would never forgive myself if I knew I could have saved him. Never!"

Joe's hands folded firmly around her shoulders.

"I'm not going to let you do this, MJ. It's too dangerous for you to be out there on your own. I think the best thing we can do now is pray for the Lord's protection over Jacob and trust that He will bring him home safely."

MJ stared into Joe's eyes. His words made perfect sense, she knew. It's what any godly woman would do in a situation like this. But somehow, MJ could not get her heart to align with her head. The yearning to take control was too big and the anger in her heart too powerful.

Wiping her tears, she tilted her chin up and looked her husband in the eye.

"I've never been that submissive wife you're always trying to mold me to, Joe. Don't try now. Jacob is my son and he needs me. If you can go back to bed and sleep peacefully, good for you. I can't."

Snatching her purse from the coat stand, she spun around and walked out the front door without looking back once.

CHAPTER EIGHTEEN

Anger lingered for a while as MJ slowly drove through the quiet streets of Weyport. She felt betrayed by Joe, let down that he didn't understand her need to protect her son, and disappointed that he didn't feel the need to be out there helping her find him. They hardly ever argued about anything, except when they disagreed over Jacob. It was as if he'd always been the thorn in Joe's side even though he would never admit it out loud. Joe was different with Teddy, more tolerant, and more loving. At first, she thought it was because of the accident, but as time went by and Jacob matured through adolescence, it became more apparent to her that Joe favored Teddy, his actual son. And Jacob had sensed it too, inwardly knowing that blood ran thicker than water. Somehow, the two of them had made a silent pact of keeping their feelings amicable and cordial, for the sake of the family.

Something she and Joe had done as a couple themselves for years. It was as if they were on autopilot, each doing what needed to be done to live up to the standards of their faith, each an example to those they thought were watching their every move. As if they had a role in a play: Joe the elder of the church and MJ the proverbial Proverbs 31 wife. Not that they didn't do it well. They did. Well enough to hide their lackluster marriage from the rest of the world and fool everyone into believing that they were the perfect little blended churchgoing family.

But not today, not now. All pretenses were left at the door when she disobeyed Joe's wishes. She couldn't care less if the church judged her for being unyielding to her husband. All that mattered was that she found her son.

Her hands gripped the steering wheel of her wood-paneled Dodge Caravan as it noisily rolled its way through the neighborhood. The van was old and had seen better days but she could never replace it. Her thoughts trailed to when she first bought it, realizing that it was also the last time she and Jacob were truly happy. They had bought the minivan shortly before Jacob's dad passed away and she got the crazy idea in her head for the three of them to take a road trip. A slight smile curled at the outer corners of her mouth as she recalled their last trip together. It was perfect. As if Jacob's dad hadn't been ill. Hadn't had a death sentence over him. Hadn't been defeated by his cancer. They were able to just lock it all away, and pretend that nothing was wrong. That nothing was going to happen. And after he died and she was forced to sell their house to pay the medical bills, the minivan was all she had left. The van... and Jacob.

She straightened her spine as she neared the skate park, her eyes searching every dark corner of the park. But as with the rest of her search, Jacob was nowhere to be found.

Uncertain of what to do next, she kept warm by keeping the van's engine running as she sat there in the dark car park. The night was cold and a shiver ran down her spine. Perhaps if Jacob was hiding beneath one of the ramps and saw her he'd come to her. She'd wait. However long it took.

IT WAS a little after four a.m. when a knock on her window startled her awake. The minivan's engine was still running when she looked over to find Angus next to her window. Slightly disorientated at first she cranked the window down and turned the vehicle off.

"Please tell me you found Jacob," she said.

Angus leaned in.

"Not yet. I take it you haven't either."

Hearing his words nearly had MJ burst into tears all over again but she held back—stayed strong.

"What about the other boy? Any news on him?" she

asked instead, hoping that he might have been found and would lead them to Jacob.

"Nothing yet either. How long have you been sitting out here?" Angus switched gears.

MJ glanced at the clock. "A few hours."

"Then there's a chance Jacob might have found his way home while you were out here."

The notion instantly sobered MJ into action and she started the car.

"You're right! He could be home. I can't believe I didn't think of that. I'll call you if he's home," she hastily replied as she clipped in her seatbelt.

Without wasting another moment, MJ threw her car in reverse, nearly backing into a lamppost. With her hopes and prayers now pinned on Jacob being sound asleep in his bed when she got home, she raced her car through the quiet streets. Barely able to contain her breathing her car screeched into the driveway. Moments later she leaped onto the porch and burst through the front door. With her purse still clutched in her hand she ran down the hallway to Jacob's room, excitement, fear, and hope now pushing onto her heart from all sides.

But it all came crashing down when she turned on the light to his bedroom only to find his bed had still not been slept in.

"No, this can't be happening! Why is this happening?" Her hands were in her hair as she dropped down on

Jacob's bed and curled herself into a ball. Every cell inside her body wanted to expel the deep anguish in her soul and suddenly she couldn't find the strength to hold it together. She buried her face inside his pillow, smelled his teenage odor, and drenched it with her tears.

It was only when Joe's hands gently settled on her back a short while later that she lifted her head, her sad eyes meeting his.

"Why is this happening, Joe? Why my Jacob? What have I ever done to God that He would punish me like this?"

Joe's voice was gentle, and as always, he spoke as if he were reading one of the trinkets from the church foyer.

"We ask not why, MJ, but trust that all things will come together in His perfect plan. You need to stand firm in faith and trust that this is all just a misunderstanding and that Jacob will be home before you know it."

Annoyance snapped into place and MJ jumped up to face him.

"Can you not just once speak to me as your wife, Joe? Without throwing the Bible at me. I know what it says. I've been preaching Romans 8:28 to all those women from the shelter for years now but this isn't the same. My son is missing, gone, possibly in trouble. I hardly think that any good can come from this."

Joe stayed seated on the bed, his temperament as calm as it always was. MJ wanted him to react, wanted him to tell her it was all going to be okay and that Jacob would be home soon. But he didn't.

She snatched her purse off the bed and wiped the tears from her face, holding back the anger that was bubbling inside her when she turned to face Joe.

"Something bad has happened to him, Joe. I can feel it. And if you want to sit here clutching the Bible instead of helping me look for him, I can't do anything about that. But I won't. I'm going to find my son if it's the last thing I do on God's green earth."

Without another glance at Joe, MJ stormed out of the room, nearly bumping into Teddy where he stood rubbing his eyes as he stared at them from the hallway. She gave him a brief hug and a kiss on his forehead.

"Don't you worry, Teddy, okay? Jacob will be home very soon."

Teddy's eyes held her gaze.

"It's the pirates, they took him."

Confusion settled into her face but she brushed it away.

"Go back to bed, Teddy. It's too early for you to be up."

"He forgot his costume. Heroes need their costumes," Teddy continued.

MJ held him by his shoulders and looked him in the eye.

"Teddy, sweetheart, I don't have time for this now. I have to go speak to the sheriff so we can find Jacob, okay?

But I'm sure Daddy would love to play dress-up with you later."

She planted another kiss on his forehead and attempted to leave when Teddy pushed one hand in front of her face, a black ski mask dangling from his pudgy fingers.

CHAPTER NINETEEN

MJ stared into her young stepson's eyes, the piece of black fabric now scrunched up in his hand. Taking it from him she unfolded it, holding the mask up to take it all in. The tiny red embroidered dragon didn't look like any clothing brand she knew of, nor did she know why Jacob would have a piece of attire only criminals would have use for considering he'd never been skiing or, as far as she was aware, had any ski trips planned.

Her heart was suddenly pounding inside her chest as she held it up to Joe before turning back to Teddy.

"Where did you get this, Teddy?" she asked.

Teddy rubbed at his eyes.

"It's Jacob's. He fights the pirates."

MJ was on one knee, her mind scrambling to make sense of Teddy's answer.

"Teddy, sweetheart, I don't understand. Does Jacob play dress-up with you?"

Teddy shook his head.

"Heroes keep secrets," Teddy announced then turned and walked back to his room.

Deciding not to probe Teddy any further, MJ walked back into Jacob's room, her eyes now suspiciously glancing around the room.

"I think you might be right, MJ. I think Jacob might be involved with something neither of us is aware of. We should tell Angus about this."

MJ's face lit with fury.

"Have you lost your mind, Joe? If, and it's a huge *if*, but if Jacob is involved with any kind of criminal activity we absolutely do not run to the sheriff with this. We might as well throw my son under a moving bus. No, we say nothing about this to anyone. For all we know this is from school. A play, or perhaps a new wrestling outfit. I'm certain there's a perfectly good explanation for it."

Joe came to stand next to her, his voice tainted with warning as he spoke.

"Let's hope you're right, MJ. But I wasn't born yesterday. Jacob hasn't quite been himself lately. And every morning at breakfast he's yawning away like he hasn't slept a wink. His grades have been slipping too. Not to mention the sudden infatuation with skateboarding. He might not be my son by blood, MJ, but I've been a father to him since he was just a toddler. He hates skateboarding.

And if there's one thing I've seen consistently among the teenagers I've counseled in all my years in the church, it's that sudden behavioral changes just like these meant only one thing. If you were honest with yourself, Mary-Jean, you would see this too."

With her husband's words echoing in her ears, MJ didn't respond as she watched him leave the room to go check up on Teddy. It was as if he had just dumped a bucket of ice over her head, robbing her of her breath which got caught in the middle of her chest. Shock rippled through her insides, her mind suddenly racing to make sense of it all before her body reacted and forced her lungs to work again. She drew in a sharp breath and felt the need to steady herself against the nearby closet.

As much as she hated to admit it, Joe was right. Jacob had been acting strange of late, secretive almost. But she had been too busy to take proper notice of him. Too busy to spend time with him. Too busy trying to make extra money to pay the mounting bills.

With her body steadied by the wall, she dropped down onto the floor, blankly staring out into the space in front of her, her insides void of any emotion, except guilt.

But guilt came in many shapes and sizes, manifesting in ways the mind didn't always fathom.

And in the mind of someone like Mary-Jean Foley, a fighter, able to bounce back and endure adversity, her guilt pushed her into motion harder than ever before.

As far as she was concerned, she only had one job in

life, and that was to protect her children, no matter the cost.

MJ pushed herself off the floor and straightened herself out before burying the ski mask inside her purse; she'd figure out how to dispose of it later. And with newfound determination, she rushed out of the house with barely a glimpse at Joe and Teddy where Joe was now snuggling Teddy up in his bed.

When her car rolled into the parking lot in front of the sheriff's office, Angus's vehicle was already parked in its spot. Impressed that he was already at his post though it wasn't yet five o'clock in the morning, she knocked on the front door. Moments later he was there to greet her.

"I thought you might come by," Angus said as he let her in. "I've got a fresh pot of coffee. Looks like you might need one."

MJ nodded then said, "I know it's early and I'm truly sorry for that, Sheriff, but something's wrong. I can feel it. Jacob isn't like other teens. He would never just run out of the house like that and not come back. I'd like for you to file that missing person's report now and send out your deputies to find my son and bring him home... please."

Angus handed her a cup of coffee and ushered her into a seat at his desk.

"I know. I'm already ahead of you, MJ." He placed a form on the desk in front of her and then handed her a pen before pointing to a spot where she needed to sign.

"I've met Jacob and I would agree with you. He

doesn't strike me as your typical teen. But, MJ, there's something you should know."

MJ's eyes locked in on his, her insides suddenly on edge as she waited for him to continue.

"I promised Jacob I wouldn't say anything but under the circumstances, I think it will be best to get everything out on the table. The first forty-eight hours of a missing person's investigation are the most crucial." He paused and studied the anguish on her face as the reality of his words struck her afresh. "I saw Jacob at the skate park the other day. There was a man, parked up in a black car. It looked as if he was there to meet Jacob."

"What man? Who was it?" MJ's voice was urgent.

"I don't know that yet but I'm looking into it. But..." he paused then continued. "I have a feeling that I might have interrupted something. Guys like them are almost always somehow involved in criminal activity."

"And you think Jacob, my Jacob knows this man? Why would you... how could you even think that, Sheriff? Jacob's not a criminal, he's a seventeen-year-old boy and he's missing!"

"I didn't say he was, MJ. All I'm saying is that I saw them in the park and Jacob tried his best to hide whatever it was they were planning on doing. And whoever the guy was couldn't wait to get out of there fast enough."

Angus leaned forward over his desk.

"Look, I'm just following the facts, exploring all the options so we can find Jacob." He fixed his gaze on her eyes. "Have you noticed anything different in Jacob's behavior of late? Anything at all? A new friend, or a new hobby, eating less?"

MJ's stomach turned as her mind instantly transported to the black ski mask in her bag and Joe's warning words.

"No, nothing," she lied as her fingers tightened around her purse.

CHAPTER TWENTY

I n the minutes that followed, Angus entered the details on his computer while an increasingly anxious MJ paced his small office. When he was finished, he pushed his chair away from his desk and looked up at her.

"There's nothing more you can do now, MJ. An alert's been sent to all the deputies in the county. For now, I'm not linking his case to the McGee boy's case. There's just not enough evidence to support it."

Angus got up and closed the gap between them.

"Go home, MJ, get some rest. I give you my word that I will prioritize finding these boys over anything else and I will do everything in my power to find Jacob. In the meantime, I need you to draw up a list of all his friends and send it through to Tammy. You can expect to have a couple of deputies knock on your door in the next few hours. They'll want access to Jacob's room and the house. I suggest you don't go near his room for now, to preserve any clues that might point us in the right direction. I will also be appointing a search team to scour the immediate surroundings of the house and the bordering woods. Stay close to the phone, just in the event you get a ransom call. If you do, you take down as much information about the call as you can: background noises, tone of voice, that type of thing, and call me right away."

MJ didn't answer him. Instead, she stared back at him, a blank expression on her face.

"MJ, did you hear me? Go home. I'll take it from here."

"You think he's been kidnapped? My boy was taken by some lunatic, the man in the black car. Is he the one that's been lurking around our neighborhood, jumping Mrs. Richardson's fence? Why would he take Jacob? It's not like we're anyone important. We don't even have any money."

Angus held up one hand.

"MJ, you need to not get ahead of yourself now. I'm not insinuating anything of the sort. Right now, we don't know any more than we did yesterday. It's really important you don't jump to any conclusions, okay? We simply don't have any substantial facts about his disappearance and until we do, you need to keep it together. For Jacob's sake. I've got this, MJ. Go home and let us handle this the right way."

When Angus was certain he'd gotten through to MJ, he walked her back to her car before he returned to his desk. In front of him, a recent school photo of Jacob was spread across his computer screen, the big red words 'MISSING' above it. Emotions tugged at his heart as Jacob's hazel eyes stared back at him. He should have followed his instincts and protected the boy. He knew when he saw that car with him at the park that something was wrong. His instincts had rung all the alarm bells in his head. Yet he did nothing. Why didn't he act sooner? What if he was too late and Jacob had been kidnapped? What if he couldn't deliver on the promises he'd made MJ?

Doubt settled into his mind as his emotions ran away with him. Frustrated and angry with himself he dropped his head into his hands. All he could do now was to do his job, to the best of his abilities, while he relied on nearly a decade's worth of experience. After all, this wasn't his first missing person's case and he'd had plenty of successes in the past.

But though he fought hard to resist his ongoing doubt, as much as his mind tried to remind him of his past victories, he also couldn't forget the statistical odds that were stacked against him.

As doubt and fear reared their ugly heads, once more he drowned them out with prayer as he took a moment to ask God for help instead. And when he was done, somewhat settled in the peace that God would guide him through the investigation, he snatched his car keys from his drawer and set off toward Jacob's school.

CHAPTER TWENTY-ONE

Driving home, MJ was on autopilot. Her mind had stayed behind in the sheriff's office, every thought pinned on what now seemed was a reality. Jacob hadn't just run away from home, or gotten lost in a mall. He was kidnapped, stolen by a psycho who had nothing but ill intentions toward him. But why? Who would do such a thing? And why *her* son?

Questions swirled around inside her head. Questions that had no answers. None of it made sense. Or did it? Might it be that the niggling feeling she was so desperately trying to keep hidden deep inside her was, in fact, a clear sign that there was far more to this than she knew? Suspicion tugged at the back of her mind and she glanced at her purse on the seat next to her. She tried to ignore what was inside but a few yards farther on, she pulled her car onto the side of the road and reached inside her handbag to take out the ski mask. Spreading it open on the steering wheel, she examined the red dragon on the side, gliding her fingers over the small insignia. As before, the logo wasn't familiar to her so she turned the mask inside out in search of the care label, only to discover it had been cut out. She sat there on the side of the road, staring out across the front of her car, her heart now unexpectedly numb. Joe was right. Jacob had been acting strange of late. Then there was the day she had found him on the porch at dawn. He had told her he went out looking for the newspaper but she knew full well she had caught him in a lie. He was hiding something. Her son had been keeping a secret, perhaps more than one.

Immediately her mind snapped to his room. If he had hidden the mask, he might be hiding something else in there. Something that might incriminate him.

With her foot already pushing down on the accelerator, she stuffed the mask back inside her purse, now eager to get home before the deputies arrived to search his room.

Panic suddenly flooded her heart, pumping new life into its chambers. She wanted more than anything for them to find her son and bring him home safely, but not if it could send him to prison.

Gripping the steering wheel with both hands, her back straightened in her seat, she raced her way through the now busy town streets. She briefly glanced at the clock on her dashboard. Joe and Teddy would be having their breakfast in the kitchen right about now. She couldn't have them see her. It would be her secret to keep. To protect her son.

Using the front door was out of bounds; Joe and Teddy would be onto her in an instant. Her mind raced to find another way in. Then it dawned on her: her bedroom window. She never slept with the window closed. That was the only way in without them seeing her.

Minutes later she turned into her street and slowed the car down. From a distance away, she saw that the driveway to her house was still empty. Parking there would be foolish though so she turned off into a small inlet on the edge of the woodland not far from the house. The small clearing was intended for dog walkers to leave their cars while they went hiking in the forest but deciding it was the perfect place to hide her car, she parked it in the dark shadows of the surrounding trees, just out of immediate sight from the road. Trailing between the trees toward her house, she stopped and hid behind a thick trunk directly opposite the house. With a clear view of her house, she remained cautious, scouting it out first. She'd have the smallest of windows before the deputies got there to search the house and decided it was now or never. Acting purely on impulse she took one deep breath before she made her move and slipped out from behind the tree before she darted across the street and along the hedge toward the side of the house. Needing to catch her breath, she briefly paused just outside her bedroom window. With care, she peeked through the window to confirm that Joe wasn't inside the room. When he wasn't, it took hardly any time before she hoisted herself in through the window, equally grateful and impressed that she still had it in her. Once inside she heard Joe and Teddy chatting away in the kitchen and slowly moved across the room and down the hallway to Jacob's room. Her hand nervously closed around the doorknob, turning it slowly to avoid the slight squeak she had been meaning to oil for a while. Moments later she stepped inside Jacob's bedroom, shutting the door with similar stealth behind her.

Her eyes danced around the room, carefully inspecting every inch of it until her eyes settled on the fish tank. It had gone green again. Instinct told her to look there first so she rushed over and peered in through the glass to inspect the contents. But nothing looked out of place, not that she had a clue what she was looking for. When she straightened up, she took a step back, her eyes now settling on the lid that sat at a slight slant. Instantly she reacted, lifting the lid away to inspect inside the tank. In the faint fluorescent light of the fish tank, MJ's fingers traced the sticky residue where something was once fixed to the inside lid with tape.

Upset rippled through her insides. The nagging feeling was now founded in truth. Jacob had indeed been keeping secrets from her.

She popped the lid back on, her eyes now darting with more vigor throughout the room. She needed to think like him, think like a teen. She fell to her knees and pressed her cheek onto the rug, her eyes now frantically searching the spaces underneath each of the shelves in the bookcase. Nothing. She turned around and walked over to his bed, sliding her hands beneath the mattress and underneath the bed frame. This too came up empty. Two brisk leaps had her fling open his closet doors before another frantic search between his clothing also turned up void. When she was just about to give up, she dropped down and rummaged through his shoes, stretching to reach his hiking boots in the back of his closet.

When she pushed her hand into the nose of one of the shoes, her fingers brushed over something unfamiliar and she tipped the shoe over, tossing the large bundle of cash out onto the floor in front of her. Surprise jolted her heart to a near standstill, her body suddenly unable to move as her mind tried to make sense of what she was seeing. The neatly rolled bundle of notes that she guessed amounted to several hundreds of dollars brought with it an entirely new set of questions. Deciding to check the other shoe, she tipped it over as well.

This time, it was horror that hooked its claws into her heart, for next to the bundle of unexplained cash, two small sachets of white powder dropped out onto the floor.

CHAPTER TWENTY-TWO

Numbed to the core, her heart weighed down with answers that suddenly came at her from all angles, MJ tried her utmost to process what she had just found. Sadness pushed into her heart. She thought she knew her son, thought he could never be capable of something as criminal as this. Not her son. Not her Jacob. *Her* son wasn't like the other teens who came from broken homes, who needed to seek purpose elsewhere, who sought belonging. Her son was loved, accepted for who he was, and perfect in her eyes. What motivation could he possibly have to want to turn to drugs?

Tears filled her eyes as guilt set in. She was so sure that she had raised him to know better. That she'd been a present mother, one that led by setting a good Christian example. She'd raised him in the church and made him say his prayers each night. Why was that not enough?

She had failed him, horribly. She had assumed too much, taken for granted that he couldn't be influenced by the ugly world they lived in. Lost touch with him because she'd been so caught up in the struggle to help pay the bills.

How wrong she was.

In the distance, she heard a knock on the front door, then Joe's feet as he shuffled toward it.

Her body jolted into the present. Snatching up the money and sachets, she stuck them inside the pockets of her pants where the money now made a fat bulge on her hip.

Voices trailed from the living room as Joe let the deputies in and she tossed Jacob's shoes back inside his closet. Unable to now leave the house the way she had entered, she hurried to Jacob's bedroom window and pushed it open with force. Not holding back she launched herself out of the window and thumped on top of the spiky rose bush several feet below. She winced as the thorns tore into her hands, ripping part of her blouse as she rolled herself off. From inside the house, the voices grew louder as they moved toward Jacob's room and she reached up to shut the window just as Joe entered the room, the deputies in tow.

Exhausted and aching all over, MJ acted quickly and sprinted along the hedge back toward the woods, the money rubbing hard against her hip. Narrowly escaping another deputy as he parked his vehicle in front of her house, she darted across the street and hid between the trees. When she finally made her way to her car she hunched down behind it to catch her breath. The money squeezed out onto the ground beside her, neatly bundled into a tube and held together with a bright red elastic band. She stared at it. Not even the rubber band looked familiar to her.

Then right away hope filled her heart and caught her off guard as another question rushed into her mind. Had Jacob been selling the drugs instead of using them? For the briefest of moments, it brought her joy to believe the former but soon the sobering thought settled into shame. Neither action was acceptable, not in the eyes of God nor the law, but if truth be told she far preferred him selling drugs to using them. That he could walk away from more easily.

She shot up an apologetic prayer, saying the words but not connecting them to her spirit. For now, she'd focus on protecting him, getting him back.

From somewhere inside the woods, a dog barked and jolted her out of her reverie. Pushing herself off the ground, she grabbed the wad of money and hurried to her car.

At first, she shoved both the money and the bags of white powder into her handbag then realized it was too risky. She couldn't chance them searching her and finding them. She glanced around the car, briefly looking into the glove box but then thought twice about that also. Perhaps she could bury them somewhere in the woods until she figured out what to do with them. Until Jacob was home safely and it all blew over.

She scanned the car for a paper bag but when she didn't find one, she yanked her satin scarf from her neck and wrapped it into a tight parcel before tying the two ends together. A quick sweep of the area around the car turned up clear and she jumped out, the satin parcel firmly clasped in her hand.

Moving quickly to where the foliage densely hugged the base of a tree that stood tall about thirty yards from the small clearing, MJ searched for a hiding spot between the leaves. It didn't take long before she found a natural hollow at the base of the tree where the roots had pushed the soil into a small moss-covered mound. Shoving the parcel inside, she covered it up with dry needles and moss and let the foliage fall back into place over the top. When she stepped back she took in the precise spot and then, using her car keys, marked the tree with a small circular etching.

When she was satisfied she had done all she could to hide the secret she now shared with her son, she ran back to her car and drove the short distance into her driveway, only to arrive as the deputies were exiting onto the porch.

Nerves on end, her stomach in knots, MJ took a deep breath as she stepped out of her car. Making every attempt to appear calm and normal, she walked toward the trio of men who were gathered on her doorstep. Behind them, Joe's brow furrowed when he saw her.

Unaware of the trickle of blood that had dried on her chin and the rip along the sleeve of her white blouse, MJ stepped onto the porch to greet them. But as she did so, Joe rushed toward her and threw his arms around her in an uncharacteristic embrace.

"It's going to be okay, MJ. They're sending a search party into the woods as we speak. Jacob will be home before we know it."

Confusion settled into MJ's mind, puzzled by Joe's strange reaction since they weren't exactly the most affectionate couple. With her body stiff against his, Joe pulled away slightly, his body blocking her from the deputies' view. In a quick sweeping motion, he wiped the blood trickle from her chin, camouflaging the action by pretending to cup her face. His eyes told MJ to play along so she let him continue the charade. By now, she recognized his cues.

"You're ice cold. Here, take my sweater," Joe continued and quickly draped his button-up sweater around her shoulders.

When done, he stood next to her, one arm draped across her shoulders while his other hand held the cardigan in place over her ripped sleeve.

"Thank you for stopping by, deputies. Please find our son and bring him home," Joe said before he bid them farewell and ushered MJ inside.

"What was that about?" MJ asked the moment Joe shut the door behind them.

"I could ask you the same thing, MJ. Have you seen what you look like?" He pointed at the dirt on her blouse along with the tear in her sleeve before taking his sweater back.

"I hadn't noticed."

She watched as Joe's face turned red.

"Well, I did, MJ, along with you climbing out of Jacob's bedroom window. I guess the rose bush will do that to you when you have to escape in a hurry."

CHAPTER TWENTY-THREE

Angus dropped the receiver back in place and pushed himself away from his desk. Dread filled his heart as his mind replayed the call he just received. He shut his eyes for a brief moment and shot up a prayer, pleading for it not to be Jacob.

A soft knock on his office door brought him back to the present and he looked up when Tammy's gentle voice came at him.

"Sorry, Sheriff, didn't mean to interrupt. The team's been dispatched. They'll meet you there. Inland Fisheries is standing by with a boat to take you out to where the body was spotted."

"Thanks, I'll be right out."

With apprehension pushing down even harder, Angus snatched up his car keys and set off to one of the waterways where he found two of his deputies talking to the local crab fisherman who had discovered the body in the salt marsh. The man was clearly shaken up but seemed more distressed about his daily catch that needed to get to the fishmonger before sunset than the dead body he found floating in the water.

"This way, Sheriff." One of the deputies broke away and led him to where the Inland Fisheries boat bobbed off a small jetty twenty yards away.

"The ME is en route, Sheriff," the Hispanic deputy said as he jumped into the boat, camera in hand.

"We'll have to get a move on with the photos before he gets here. I want the body out of the water before the news gets out. What do we know so far, Miguel?" Angus probed his deputy.

"Not much, and incidentally, Sheriff, it's a she, not a he."

Angus lifted one brow as he prompted Miguel for an explanation.

"The ME, it's a female. Just thought I'd let you know."

"Good to know, Miguel. Since you're in such a sharing mood, how about you tell me what you've learned from your interview with our man over there?" Angus lifted his chin toward the fisherman on the shore, eager to stick to the case.

"Of course, Sheriff. The guy was out on his skiff catching crab when he saw the body floating at the edge of the marsh. He went over, poked at it with his net, and immediately called it in."

"Did he see anything suspicious? Another boat perhaps or anyone else hanging around."

"Nothing, but he was very sure it wasn't here this morning. Apparently, this is his favorite spot. He comes here every day. First thing in the morning to drop his cages and back in the afternoon to pull them up."

"And he's positive the body wasn't here this morning. Perhaps he made a mistake with the location."

"He has no doubt whatsoever. Says he's been fishing here since his childhood. Knows the water like the back of his hand."

"I see. Let's make sure we get every little detail from our fisherman before we let him go. I want exact timelines. The ME's report will take too long and I want to jump on this pronto."

"Got it, Sheriff," the deputy acknowledged before he radioed the instruction through to his partner.

Angus turned to the skipper.

"Could the tides have carried the body in during the day?"

"Normally, yes, but your fisherman missed the slack tide this morning and by the sounds of it, he dropped his nets during the first high tide. The second high tide isn't until much later today. If you ask me, there is only one way the body could have ended up this far out in the salt marsh, especially between the time the fisherman dropped his nets and now. Someone moved the body and dumped it here."

Angus pondered the thought. If this was indeed a homicide and the body was brought here, it meant they didn't have a crime scene to investigate. And without a crime scene, the evidence might not be sufficient to lead them to the murderer. He scratched the back of his head as the boat slowed down and neared the water's edge to where the body floated face down in the water. As they pulled up next to it, Angus clenched his jaw, his stomach flipping with angst.

Next to him, his deputy had already started capturing the scene with his camera, oblivious to the weight that lay heavily on Angus's shoulders. He wanted desperately to turn the body over, to see the victim's face, to see if it was Jacob. But he held back, forced to wait until his deputy was finished photographing it.

"Make sure you get every angle on film, Miguel. I don't want to miss a thing."

The deputy followed through on the order and continued snapping away while Angus took it all in.

The body was definitely male, roughly Jacob's height, and wearing black jeans and a faded black hoodie with the words 'Anarchy Rules' printed in gold on the back. His eyes lingered on the design, vague familiarity tugging at his memory.

"Clearly the guy likes his music. Not my taste but hey, the kids these days listen to the weirdest things," Miguel commented as he zoomed in on it with his camera.

Angus frowned.

"Care to fill me in?"

"His sweater, it's the name of a punk rock band. The kids are going crazy for them right now. Total trash if you ask me. They performed live at The Grande about six months ago."

"The casino, out on fifty-two?"

"Yup, every young adult in a hundred-mile radius flooded to it. Apparently, the tickets sold out in hours. The casino hit an all-time high with all the feet that came through their doors. So did the crime. We had our hands full with anarchy in the real sense of the word. Everything from car theft to bar fights and even a few card counters trying their luck."

Angus studied the logo on the hoodie.

"So this guy most likely attended the concert."

"I'd say that was highly likely. These hoodies were sold exclusively at the event as far as I remember. The ones with the gold insignia were limited edition. They cost a small fortune. I only know this because my nephew lives upstate and begged me to get him one. They were long sold out by the time I got to the front of the line but even if I got there in time, I wouldn't have been able to afford it on my wage. They charged nearly a thousand dollars for it! Crazy right?"

"Which begs the question: how did our victim here afford that price tag?"

Miguel shrugged his shoulders as he snapped a few more pics as the boat changed position around the body.

"That ought to do it, Sheriff," Miguel announced after a while.

Angus didn't react instantly. His mind was too busy building a profile from the little he had gathered thus far.

"Sheriff, I think I've got enough photos. Shall we turn him over?" Miguel prompted again.

Fully present now, Angus agreed and readied himself for the worst before they pulled the body into the boat next to them. When they turned it over onto its back the young victim's face came into full view and Angus found himself staring into a pair of lifeless eyes.

CHAPTER TWENTY-FOUR

Questions scrambled inside MJ's mind while a big ball of knots dropped into her stomach. How had Joe seen her escape through Jacob's window? And how would she explain why she'd found it necessary to sneak in and out of the house, poking around in Jacob's room? Struggling to come up with an excuse, she walked into the kitchen to wash her hands, Joe close on her heels.

His eyes were big and scrutinizing from where he now stood in front of MJ.

"Must I drag it out of you, MJ? Where were you and why were you sneaking around in Jacob's room?"

"It's nothing, okay. I just couldn't face anyone."

"Nonsense and you know it. In all the years I've known you, MJ, you've never been one to shy away from anyone. You're the one person on this planet who can make small talk with anyone no matter what mood you're in. Tell me the truth, MJ. What were you doing in Jacob's room?"

MJ turned away to dry off her hands, her insides shaking under her husband's heated inquiry.

"Fine, I'll tell you. I removed the ski mask, the one Teddy gave us."

It was partially true, she justified inside her head, except it wasn't, because, at the time, she already had it inside her purse.

"Why? I thought you said it probably had to do with his wrestling clothes."

"I never said that. I have no idea where the mask came from. All I know is it looks like something criminals might wear and I didn't want them to find anything that might cast suspicion on my son."

"So you snuck into his room and removed it. What if it holds an important clue that could lead us to where he might be? Have you thought about that? Withholding information could impede their investigation, MJ."

She hadn't thought of it, her heart suddenly heavy again as she wondered if she should instead turn everything over to Angus. She brushed the notion away. It was too late now. She had come too far to rat out her son. For a brief moment, she contemplated telling Joe about what she had found and that she buried it in the woods but the look on his face told her he wouldn't understand.

"I don't know what Jacob has been up to, MJ, but I

have the sinking feeling that it's something illegal. And if he is breaking the law and the church finds out, we lose everything. Our home, our reputation, income, everything I've worked for! And I'm sure I don't need to ask you how you think we'll be able to pay Teddy's medical bills because we simply won't be able to. Unless, of course, the entire county suddenly needs plastic storage containers."

Joe's words sliced into her soul. There it was. Joe Foley, respected elder of the church and upstanding pillar of the community was more concerned about his reputation and the bills than her son. She wanted to shout at him, lay her hand across his pudgy cheek for choosing to be loyal to himself instead of to his wife and her son. Not to mention the belittling of the sideline job she did in an effort to help pay the bills. Their marriage was a sham, a silent arrangement made years ago. He needed a mother for his disabled son and she needed someone to provide for them and be a father figure to Jacob. Except he hadn't been either. All Joe Foley cared about was his church reputation and whether they portrayed the image of a perfect little Christian family. It was as if his entire identity was caught up in what people might think of them.

And all she cared about was bringing Jacob home.

Unable to look at Joe she held back her emotions, her heart bitter with resentment toward him.

But instead of spitting back at her husband, she chose the easy route, the one the two of them had managed to master to perfection over their ten-plus years of marriage every time they locked horns over something. They switched into make-believe mode, pretended that everything was fine, swept their differences under the rug, and buried their heads in the sand. And right now falling back on this tactic suited her perfectly. Her flawed marriage came second to finding her son and bringing him home.

"Where's Teddy?" She glanced toward the living room where he'd normally be watching his television programs.

"He's fine. I took him over to Jason and Ann's down the road. I didn't want him here when they searched the house. Marley and May had their puppies a few days ago so it should entertain him for a few more hours so I can get some work done."

Sarcasm dripped off his tongue as he slung the hint her way.

"Let me not stop you then. I'm going to get cleaned up. I'll scoop Teddy up on my way back from stopping by the sheriff's office."

"You will do nothing of the sort, MJ! Have you not done enough already? Let the sheriff do his job and you do yours. We don't need the entire town gossiping about our business."

"And what business is that exactly, Joe? Newsflash! My son is missing and you've done absolutely nothing to help me find him except protect your so-called church reputation. Is that all you're worried about, Joe? What other people might think? What about Jacob? What about the fact that he might be missing, or worse, dead? Or would that be a relief to you?" Her heart broke as she said it.

Joe's eyes narrowed.

"You're understandably emotional about all of this, MJ, but you're not thinking clearly. Let's face the truth here. Jacob's changed, he's different, more inward, secretive even. He has been for a while now. We don't know who his friends are or who he hangs out with at school. Heck, we don't even know if he has any friends since none of the ones we thought were his friends have seen him in weeks. We don't really know Jacob at all anymore."

MJ's body stiffened.

"That's because you don't want to and from where I'm standing it's very clear you don't know me either, Joe."

The bitter words rolled off her tongue far too easily and she watched Joe's face as the words took effect.

When he finally spoke his voice was dejected, cracking as he said, "I guess I don't, MJ. But then it seems neither of us knows each other at all anymore."

With nothing more to say between them, MJ brushed past Joe as she made her way to their bedroom, stopping midway when the phone suddenly rang.

Joe got to the phone first and MJ watched from the end of the hallway, her eyes fixed on his face as he listened to the voice on the other end of the phone. When seconds later his eyes darted to hers, she knew something was wrong. She hastened toward him and stood closer to try to listen in.

"Who is it? What's happening? Is it Jacob?" The questions rolled off her tongue, their spat forgotten for the moment.

"Thank you for letting us know, Sheriff," Joe said before he put the receiver back in place.

Fear ran cold inside her as MJ waited for Joe to tell her what was going on. His face was grim and far too serious when he looked up at her.

"You're scaring me, Joe! What's going on?"

"They found a body down in the salt marsh."

A gasp escaped from MJ's mouth before it wedged inside her heart.

"Whose? Is it Jacob? Tell me!"

"It's the McGee boy."

"And Jacob? Was he with him?"

"They don't know anything yet. Angus says his deputies are scouring the area as we speak but so far, there's nothing to indicate that they even knew each other or that the two cases are linked. All we can do now is wait. Angus assured me that they're doing everything in their power to find Jacob."

"But what if Jacob..." She couldn't finish the sentence. Instead, she sank onto the nearby sofa, her palms covering her mouth as she stared blankly into the space in front of her.

"You can't let your head run away with you now. You've forgotten that your son ran out of the house entirely of his own accord. The child ran away because he's obviously hiding something. Teens do that and then suddenly they walk through the front door as if nothing ever happened. Mark my words. Jacob is probably out there watching the house from behind one of those trees. He'll be back and then we'll be left with egg on our faces for causing all this commotion."

Having said all there was to say, a grumpy Joe turned and walked into his office, shutting the door behind him.

MJ remained on the sofa, her body strangely numb while her mind tried to process all that had just been said and happened. As she sat there quietly on her own, her eyes fell and lingered on the small pottery dish in the nearby bookcase. Jacob had made it for her one Mother's Day. It was another stark reminder of how much she stood to lose and where her loyalties truly lay.

CHAPTER TWENTY-FIVE

As expected, the news of his only son's death hit him hard. The grief lay bare in the deep lines on his face as Ray McGee turned away from Angus and shut the door to his trailer behind him without so much as speaking a single word.

Angus had intended on asking him a few more questions, but it was clear Ray wasn't in any condition to be interviewed. He was the kind of man who needed time on his own to come to terms with it.

Sympathy lay heavy in Angus's heart where he stood staring out across the trailer park. He turned his attention heavenward and pleaded with God to spare him having to make another house call like the one he had just made to Aaron McGee's father. As he spoke with God, he thanked Him that it was Joe who answered his earlier call instead of MJ. She would not have been so easily accepting that he was still nowhere closer to finding her son.

The thought of having to make another house call, possibly next time to Jacob's mother, broke his heart into a million pieces. Informing parents that they'd lost a child never got any easier and it was the part of his job he hated the most. Over his years in law enforcement, he'd had his fair share of delivering bad tidings to loved ones but never to someone he shared lunch, or his faith, with. Delivering such news to MJ would be far worse than any call he'd ever made before. This time it was personal. He'd seen the desperation in her eyes, seen how much her son meant to her, seen how far she'd go to save him. There was nothing MJ wouldn't do to save her son. And he would know. He'd seen it all before. In his own mother's eyes, that night she packed their bags and the three of them ran away from his abusive father. She had somehow managed to save up enough money to pay their airfare. 'A single trip to anywhere,' she had called it. And when they got to the airport, it just so happened that the next flight out of Glasgow took them straight to Las Vegas.

Perhaps that was what he liked about MJ. She shared the same resilience as his own mother. That and the fact that she too had ginger hair, just like his mother did before it turned white.

A faint smile broke across his face as his memory flooded with pictures of his mother when he and his brother were just children. Images of them visiting his grandparents in Scotland when he was barely twelve. It had been the only time they went back to Scotland; to bid her father farewell before he passed.

Emotions tugged hard at his heart as Angus stared across the open land, the big orange sun hanging low on the horizon as he vowed to do whatever it took to find Jacob Foley.

Still deep in thought, Angus barely heard Ray's croaky voice drifting in the breeze toward him. It was only when Ray spoke directly behind him that he snapped out of his trance.

"Are you coming in or not, Sheriff?"

Angus spun around to see Ray already headed back inside his trailer. He found Ray seated at the kitchen table, a bottle of expensive whiskey open in front of him. Wondering how it was that Ray could afford such an expensive bottle on his wage Angus sat down opposite him. He must have stared at the bottle too long because Ray was quick to shove an empty glass in front of him.

"Want one?" he offered.

"I'm not much of a drinker, thanks."

"You should try. It numbs the pain. Works like magic, every time."

Angus wanted to tell him that Jesus would go further but he held back. There was too much anger behind Ray's eyes.

"Looks like an expensive bottle," Angus fished.

"One of the best, a limited edition too. My boy had good taste and he took great care of me."

"So Aaron bought it for you?"

"Every week like clockwork. He was a good boy." Ray's voice broke as he said it and he threw back another mouthful as his eyes welled up with fresh tears.

"Are you okay with me asking you a few questions about him?"

"A lot of good that will do now, Sheriff, but sure, fire away."

Ray made a rough swipe across his face with his sleeve before Angus continued.

"You said before that he did a few odd jobs after school. Would you know where his most recent job was?"

Ray shuffled uncomfortably before topping up his glass.

"I don't know."

Something about the way he said it told Angus he was lying.

"I'd like to catch the guy who did this to your son, Ray. If you know anything, anything at all that can help me find his killer, you can tell me."

Ray shuffled in his seat again, avoiding eye contact as he spoke again.

"I told you, Sheriff, he worked all over the place. I didn't exactly keep track of his jobs. You sure you don't want one of these?" Ray tipped the liquor bottle toward Angus as he said it.

Ray was deflecting and Angus wasn't going to have it. He had Jacob to think about.

"Do you know if Aaron knew a boy called Jacob Foley?"

Ray's eyes narrowed before he answered.

"I heard about the boy. He went missing a couple days ago."

"Correct, and I'd like to find him before he ends up in the salt marsh too."

It was a low blow, Angus knew, but he had to push Ray a little harder.

"And what makes you think my Aaron had anything to do with his disappearance, huh, Sheriff? I already told you, Aaron was a good boy. He did nothing wrong."

"No one said he did, Ray. I'm simply trying to find out if they knew each other. If perhaps they might have been abducted by the same person."

Ray took another swig before he spoke again, the liquor splashing from his lips as he did so.

"As far as I know they rode the school bus together and hung out at the skate park in town a few times. But that's all I know. I don't know what Aaron did while I played the slots, Sheriff. Maybe you should ask this Jacob boy's parents."

Ray was slurring his words and Angus knew he had gotten as much out of Ray McGee as his liquor would allow.

Just then, a knock at the door announced the timely

arrival of two of his deputies and Angus jumped up to let them in.

"I'll be off now, Ray. I would appreciate it if you let my deputies have access to your son's room. Every bit of evidence could help us find the guy who did this. I might have a few more questions for you tomorrow so don't leave town. If you think of anything else that could help us find the Foley boy, I'd appreciate your call, please. And again, I am deeply sorry for your loss. I will do whatever I can to bring his murderer to justice."

As Angus turned toward the door, he leaned in to whisper to one of his deputies.

"This guy is hiding something. Make sure you go through the boy's room with a fine-tooth comb. And if you manage to get anything else out of him before he passes out, let me know. Ray McGee knows far more than he's letting on."

CHAPTER TWENTY-SIX

E xhaustion had taken its toll on Angus and he downed the drive-thru coffee in a few swigs. He had been out with his deputies all night scouring the areas around the salt marsh and the woods adjacent to the Foley house. Only to find no further evidence or any clues as to how Aaron's body had ended up in the salt marsh, or where Jacob was. It was as if the town did everything in its power to cover up its wickedness. As if somehow Pete Hutchinson still held the town captive with his evil betrayal.

As he sat outside the medical examiner's office, he glanced at his watch. 8:27 a.m. With any luck, or divine intervention, he would walk away having established at least the cause of death. God knows he needed answers. He was no closer to finding anything substantial to go on that would help him solve either case. And that wasn't doing anyone any good.

It had been barely four months since he took over as sheriff, and apart from a few petty thefts, this was his first major case. Tension tugged at the back of his neck and he rubbed at it with one hand. Two bodies in less than six months wouldn't go down well with the district attorney.

AARON MCGEE'S body lay bare atop the medical examiner's table when Angus walked in a few minutes later.

"You must be the new sheriff in town." A lanky brunette looked up from her clipboard and greeted him as he walked in.

"Angus Reid, nice to meet you."

"Murphy Delaney." She shook his hand.

"You have perfect timing, Sheriff Reid. I was about to call your office. I thought you might have urgency around this case so I pulled an all-nighter."

"That's great to hear. You're the ME then?" Angus tried hiding the surprise on his face. His last medical examiner was a standoffish introverted man who mostly spoke with his eyes. Murphy was the exact opposite.

"I am, Sheriff Reid." She flashed a mysterious smile that sent a jolt through his stomach.

"Nice to meet you and you can call me Angus." He paused briefly before he continued. "Hopefully you've got something for me to go on. Time is fast running out on finding the Foley boy alive."

"I've heard about the missing teen. You think the two cases are linked?" she asked.

"I don't have proof of it but my gut says they are, yes. Any chance you've got a cause of death for me on our young deceased friend here yet?"

"Even though I haven't had much time to examine him properly"—her eyes smiled at Angus—"I might be able to offer you a few leads to go on, yes. As it happens, I can tell you the cause of death was undoubtedly asphyxiation."

"So he did drown."

"Nope, he was dead before he hit the water. By my estimation, I'd say a good ten to twelve hours at least. My guess is they were trying to dispose of the body, hoping for it to sink. Of course, it did at the time but as post-mortem changes set in putrefaction produced enough gases to make it buoyant. Most likely the tide brought him out to the salt marsh."

Angus frowned.

"He suffocated. I don't see any bruises around his neck. If he didn't drown and he wasn't strangled, how is asphyxia the cause?"

"How observant of you, Sheriff. I'm guessing this isn't your first soiree around a homicide investigation table." Murphy flashed him another smile.

Angus couldn't help but notice how attractive she was.

"You guessed right. I had my fair share up in Clark County."

"So you're from Nevada? How fun." She was joking as she said it. "I've only been to Vegas once. Can't say I enjoyed the desert setting. Give me a quiet coastal spot like this any day."

She pulled on a pair of latex gloves and leaned over the corpse to pick up his arm, lifting it for Angus to get a better view.

"See this? Puncture wounds. I'm still waiting on the tox report but I'm fairly certain it was a drug overdose."

Angus skimmed the body before his gaze settled on Aaron's face.

"Dare I ask if it was self-inflicted?" he said still staring at Aaron's pale but peaceful face.

Again, Murphy smiled at him, ostensibly impressed with his insight. She rested the arm back in place before pointing at the start of several post-mortem bruises on Aaron's shoulders.

"He put up a brave fight but based on these contusions on both his shoulders as well as around his wrist, I'd say he was held down and injected."

A sick feeling churned deep inside Angus's stomach, silently praying that Jacob wasn't dealt the same fate.

"Are you able to say exactly how long he was dead before he hit the water? It might help us narrow the search for the scene of the crime."

"My initial guess is that it was no more than a few

hours but it's difficult to say without the tox results. Once I have those, I can compare them to the findings of my internal exam."

"Thanks, Murphy. I'd appreciate a copy of that toxicology report the moment you have it, please. And if anything else pops up, please do let me know."

"Sure will, Angus. I hope for both our sakes you find the Foley boy. It's never easy examining the young ones."

Angus nodded in agreement.

"I'm doing everything I can to avoid that, Murphy. If you can get me that report as soon as you can, I'd really appreciate it."

She saluted him in reply as he left, a spark of something unfamiliar lingering between them.

The drive back to his office took a detour past the salt marsh where Aaron's body was discovered the day before. Their search during the night had been fruitless, leaving in its wake nothing but questions. In its stead, yellow police tape flapped in the breeze, leaving nothing but an empty stretch of salt marsh fenced in between the taped lines. As if nothing had ever happened. As if the marsh held onto its secrets to annoy him even more.

Frustration lay shallow and he struggled to contain the emotions that threatened to have him yell it out across the barren marsh. It was bad enough that the McGee boy had died on his watch but having it happen to Jacob wasn't an option.

Angus lingered in his car for a while, looking out

across the calm ocean. If only it could speak. Perhaps he'd be closer to finding out who in his town was evil enough to rob a young man of his life only to then dump his body in the ocean. As his mind lingered on the few facts he had gathered so far, his deliberation entwined in conversation with God, and a sudden revelation pierced through. Whoever dropped Aaron's body out at sea must have had a boat to do so.

Adrenaline pushed into his veins and had him turn his car's nose back onto the road. He raced toward the marina, kicking dirt up as he did so. A newfound fire burned inside his belly as he glanced at the clock on his dashboard. It had been nearly forty-eight hours since Jacob Foley ran out of his house. By most accounts, it would already be too late. Rejecting the doubt that suddenly flooded his heart, he forced the negativity out of his mind and recited Zechariah 4:6 out loud.

"Not by might, nor by power but by my Spirit, says the Lord of hosts."

Again he spoke the scripture out loud, his voice growing louder and more urgent as he recited it several times over, praying it as much as demanding it into being. He needed to say it aloud. Needed to remind himself to lean on God. To drown out the doubt, the fear, the dread that had built up inside him. To find Jacob before it was too late.

CHAPTER TWENTY-SEVEN

When Angus arrived at the marina, his faith restored to power, conviction intact that he would not only find Jacob Foley in time but also that he would find whoever killed Aaron McGee, he set off toward the marina manager's office.

As he stepped into the marina manager's office, he found a short, thickset man sitting behind a messy desk, his mouth stuffed with half an egg mayo sandwich when he greeted Angus.

"What can I do you for, Sheriff?" Half-chewed food crumbled down onto the desk in front of him.

"Didn't mean to interrupt your late breakfast but I was hoping I could have a look at your manifest covering the past two or three days."

The manager leaned back in his chair, his large tummy

pushing out against his desk as he wiped the food deeper into his beard with a paper napkin.

"Anything, in particular, you're looking to find, Sheriff?"

The man's demeanor showed signs of hostility, which raised suspicion in Angus.

"Just a case I'm investigating." He intentionally paused and waited to see how the manager was going to play it out.

Instead of answering, he shoved the other half of his sandwich into his mouth and added a mouthful of coffee, taking his time to react to Angus's request.

Angus waited, his eyes instead taking in every inch of the small office. When it settled on a large corkboard on the wall over the manager's shoulder, the guy suddenly jumped to his feet, casting yet again a cloud of suspicion over him.

"Normally, I'd insist you bring me the proper paper-work, Sheriff, but since this is our first acquaintance, I'll cut you some slack."

He picked up a clipboard from one corner of his desk and handed it to Angus, his body deliberately trying to block the corkboard behind him.

"It's all there. If you tell me what you're looking for I can speed this up. I don't enjoy my coffee cold."

Angus studied the man's face. It was clear there was something on the corkboard he didn't want Angus to see. Turning his attention to the manifest in his hand, Angus skimmed through the entries. According to the timelines, there were only two boats that left the marina, both fishing trawlers, and their departure and return times didn't align with Murphy's estimate of when Aaron's body got dumped in the water.

"Were there any other boats that came through here that you might have accidentally left off this manifest?"

The manager's face went red.

"Are you insinuating that I'm not doing my job properly, Sheriff?"

"I don't know. Are you?"

Angus deliberately aimed his question at striking a nerve. Time was of the essence.

"Look, Sheriff, you are clearly new to how things are done here in Weyport. I've been the marina manager for a very long time. Longer than you've been on this earth and trust me, I know who comes in and out of my marina at all times. I don't need a piece of paper to confirm it. Around here, we take each other at our word. It's all about relationships and looking out for each other. We take care of one another, if you know what I mean."

The man's eyes lingered on Angus, his eyebrows raised.

Ignoring the hint, Angus shifted his gaze back toward the corkboard behind him.

"Then, since we're here taking care of each other, you won't mind telling me about those boats you've got logged on that board behind you. By the looks of it, it seems you're running a separate manifest to the one in my hand. And if I'm not mistaken, it looks like two of those logs coincide with the dates in my inquiry's timeline. Any particular reason why they aren't listed here?" Angus dropped the paper manifest on the table in front of him, deliberately covering the man's sandwiches.

The gesture wasn't appreciated, evident in the manner by which the manager yanked it off his lunch before he tossed it to one side.

"Like I said, Sheriff, I've done you a courtesy by showing you my manifest without you giving me the proper papers to divulge my clients' private affairs. Now if you'll excuse me, I would like to finish my brunch while my coffee is still warm."

But Angus had dealt with people like him before. The man was defensive and it was clear it had something to do with what was written on the wall behind him. He stole another look at the corkboard, memorizing the two names that fell within his timeline before he said, "I realize this is the first time we're meeting, but you should know some-thing about me; I am very good at my job and when a body washes up on my shore and a teen goes missing, I make it my business to find whoever is responsible. And if that means I arrive at your door without the *proper papers*, so be it. Now, as a word of warning, if I find out that you intentionally manipulated your manifest to hide informa-tion that might lead to me finding these criminals, or worse, you are involved in it in any way, shape, or form, your next sandwich and cold coffee will be served from inside prison walls."

Angus held his gaze before he turned to leave.

"I hope you're not threatening me, Sheriff. Like I said, I've been in this town longer than you've been alive. I know a lot of people and we don't take kindly to threats like those, even from an officer of the law."

Angus held back any reaction as he walked toward the door. Then, stopping briefly in the doorway, he spoke over his shoulder.

"There's a new sheriff in town, sir, and I will do whatever it takes to find my man. I take care of my town too, if you know what I mean."

And with his final words spoken, Angus left the marina manager's office and set off toward the moorings, walking along the jetties between the boats. His eyes skimmed over the near dozen moored boats, his attention set on finding the two names on the corkboard. When his search turned up empty, he made his way back to his car. As he passed around the back of the manager's office, he heard him talking on the phone and hung back beside the open window.

"I'm telling you, man, this guy is sharp. He's not like Hutch. You better watch your back." Angus heard him say before the manager continued. "Yes, I'll be here, but after tonight, I'm lying low until all this is over. Just take care of it, okay?"

The receiver slammed down on the phone as he hung up, swearing under his breath as he did so.

With his instincts confirmed, Angus assessed his next move. For a brief instant, he contemplated approaching the manager about what he had overheard him say, but then sense took over. He'd wait it out and come back later, stake out the marina, and follow him. Whatever the manager agreed to do that evening might very well lead Angus straight to finding Jacob.

CHAPTER TWENTY-EIGHT

Back at his office, Angus found Murphy's full report waiting for him on his desk. Anxious tension tugged at his insides as he eagerly shifted behind his desk and flipped the folder open. Color images of Aaron McGee's body spread out across the desk, a few pictures zooming in on the large dragon tattoo on his chest. Moving his attention to the written sheets of paper, he skimmed over the details of the report, eager to find the part where it might tell him the exact time Aaron died before his killer tossed his body overboard. A few pages into the report a section of bold text jumped out at him. It showed his time of death was estimated to be at the same time he hit the water.

"That's not possible," he said to himself.

"What isn't?" Murphy's voice suddenly cut through his thoughts.

When he looked up, she was standing in his doorway.

"Let me guess." She smiled before he could say anything, "You're baffled about his T.O.D., right? I figured you might be which is why I thought I'd pop by to help you out."

Angus gestured for her to sit down opposite him, his frown turning into a soft smile.

"You are absolutely correct. It doesn't make any sense."

"That depends on which way you look at it. You're acting under the assumption that he was killed somewhere on land and then carried onto a boat before he got tossed in the ocean."

She paused, waiting for Angus to piece it together.

"Except he wasn't. He was killed on the boat. Of course!" Angus exclaimed in elation as the penny dropped. "That makes perfect sense. He was taken out to sea first, then killed on the boat and immediately thrown overboard."

"You're welcome," Murphy said, smiling as she sat back in her chair.

"I owe you, Murphy, thank you. It's the first possible break in the case."

"I'd take all the credit but unfortunately I can't. I cheated."

His brows furrowed in a frown as his head cocked to one side.

"Read on, here." She pointed at a paragraph on the same sheet of paper and Angus studied the notes.

"Wood fragments! You found wood fragments under his fingernails." His voice was laden with excitement.

"Yup, not just any wood, the kind you typically find on a boat. But wait, there's more." She mocked the television commercials. "I took the liberty of sending it off to a friend of mine in forensics who put a rush on it for me." Her eyes smiled at him as she said it. "It contained paint compounds, royal blue pigment to be precise." She got to her feet and stood next to her chair. "You're looking for a boat that is either entirely blue or has some component of it painted with a royal blue paint, maybe its deck or even the railing. That's your crime scene."

Excitement threatened to explode in his chest as the information filtered through him. He was up on his feet now too, pacing the space behind his desk with one hand on his hip while the other rubbed at the nape of his neck.

"That's the best news I've heard all week. I was starting to think I would never catch a break. Not in this case and certainly not in this town either."

"Sometimes, all it takes is a little bit of faith, Sheriff," Murphy said as she turned and walked toward the door. "You're doing a great job, Angus. It's about time a man of honor runs this town. Shout if you need anything else," she yelled back over her shoulder as she left.

A smile broke on Angus's face as he remained standing behind his desk, his gaze fixed on the report in front of him. In the quiet of his heart he thanked God for the breakthrough, for putting his investigation back on course, for bringing him one step closer to finding Aaron's killer, and for using Murphy to do it. As his prayer ended with a plea for Jacob to still be alive, Tammy interrupted him from where she stood halfway in his doorway.

"Sorry to barge in like this, Sheriff, but I've got Mrs. Foley out front. She's insisting on see—"

MJ burst past her into the office before Tammy could finish her sentence and went to stand opposite Angus at his desk.

"I want answers, Angus. It's been two days and you are nowhere closer to finding my boy."

"Sorry, Sheriff," Tammy apologized before leaving his office.

"Take a seat, MJ," he said.

"I don't want to take a seat, Angus! I want answers. I demand you tell me what you're doing to find my boy. Please, you have to find him! He's still out there somewhere and you're hiding in here behind your desk!" Her eyes were filled with angst as she slumped down in the chair opposite him.

"I'm doing everything I can to find him, MJ. I've had teams scouring the woods next to your house around the clock, keeping me abreast of it every hour. They're bringing a K-9 unit in as we speak. They are bound to notice Jacob's trail. I gave you my word that finding Jacob is at the top of my priority list and I won't stop until I do."

As he spoke, MJ's eyes fell on the open folder in front

of him, the enlarged image of a dragon tattoo holding her gaze captive.

Angus slammed the folder shut.

"Sorry, you shouldn't have seen those."

"Is that the McGee boy?" she asked, her voice subdued.

"It is, yes, but we can't assume Jacob's case is linked with his. Right now we're treating them as two separate cases and it's important that you do the same."

He still wanted to encourage her to go home and that he would keep her posted but MJ was already on her feet, her hands clutching her purse to her chest.

"I have to go, sorry. I'll let you get on with it then."

Stunned over her abrupt departure, Angus watched as MJ rushed out of his office without saying another word. Moments later, Tammy popped her head around his door.

"Sorry, Sheriff, I tried to stop her but she was, as always, so persistent. Although I will say she looked more upset when she left. Is everything okay?"

Angus let out a heavy sigh.

"I think she got a bit of a shock. Unfortunately, she saw the McGee boy's photos before I had a chance to put them away."

"That explains it. Shall I be more assertive with her next time?"

"No, let her be. She's going through a lot right now. Besides you wouldn't be able to stop her if you tried."

"Copy that, Sheriff." Tammy nodded in agreement before she shut the door behind her as she left.

Angus dropped down in his chair and spread the photos across his desk once again, poring over them in the hope that he'd find another lead to go on. When he turned up nothing else, he checked in with the search team before he made one final call to the boatyard.

But even after asking three different people if they had ever seen or repaired a boat that had been painted with blue paint, his call only left him with more questions than answers. Something that by now he should have grown used to whenever he tried to get any information from the townsfolk. It was as if they had an invisible pact between them. The very one the stocky marina manager had alluded to earlier.

CHAPTER TWENTY-NINE

MJ's heart pounded hard inside her chest as she stormed out of the sheriff's office. She slipped in behind the wheel of her car. With both hands extended on the steering wheel, she pushed her head back against the headrest and squeezed her eyes tight, every muscle in her body now taut with fear. She had recognized the dragon on Aaron McGee's body the instant she saw it. It was an exact match to the one found on Jacob's ski mask.

She must have seen wrong or made a mistake so she shoved her hands inside her purse and pulled the mask out onto her lap.

But there was no mistake. The small red dragon insignia was identical to the tattoo on Aaron McGee's chest.

Fear suddenly pushed the air out of her lungs and she

fought hard to steady her breathing. Desperate for air she leaped from her car, her fist still wrapped around the mask. With one hand leaning on the hood of her car, bent at the waist as she struggled for air, she fought the panic that clutched at her insides. When after several minutes she was finally able to breathe again, she threw her head back and pushed her face into the dim sunlight. But panic had taken up residence within her thoughts instead, her emotions once more running rampant inside her chest.

This can't be happening. It wasn't possible. Not her Jacob! He couldn't be part of a gang, wouldn't be. There had to be a mistake. Perhaps the McGee boy dropped it and Jacob picked it up, or maybe it was all just a coincidence. Yes, that must be it, a coincidence.

But though her mind tried its utmost to provide her with an explanation, she instinctively knew the shocking truth. And as her heart tried to come to terms with it, her determination to keep her son's secrets forced its way to the front of her mind.

Sudden clarity pushed through the fear and panic when a car pulled up a few bays away and pulled her into the present. Drawing attention to herself was the last thing she needed right now. Having to explain the mask in her hand while she was trying to protect her son would be nearly impossible to do. So, she got back into her car and headed home.

But, after several blocks farther, images of her son lying on a steel table in the morgue plagued her. Tightness increased in her chest and she pulled her car off to the side of the road. Thoughts of her son's body washing up some- where like the McGee boy's nagged at her emotions and vomit sat shallow in her throat. She couldn't let that happen, wouldn't let that happen. Not now, not ever.

As MJ Foley drew in a deep breath to calm her nerves and shoved the mask back into the corner of her purse, she knew exactly what she needed to do.

DOGS BARKED FURIOUSLY in the distance as MJ pulled up next to the woodland clearing near her house. She had intended on digging up the rest of Jacob's secrets but as she looked back into the small parking area, it was entirely taken over by search and rescue workers. Several vehicles ranging from county deputies to state police and forest services were squashed into the small space. Scat- tered between them, a small group of men stood poring over a map on the hood of one of the cars while another small group huddled nearby, their search and rescue dogs at their heels.

MJ bit down on her lip. They were all there for one reason alone and that was to find her son. That should have been a good thing. But at that moment, all she could think about was the small parcel she had hidden inside the cavity of a tree and what would happen if they found it.

As she sat there contemplating how to get to it before

they did, one of the men broke away from the group. By the time she realized he was walking directly toward her, it was too late and his knuckles rapped on her passenger-side window. Nerves twitched inside as she leaned over and rolled the window down.

"You can't park here, ma'am," the young Hispanic deputy said with a stern voice.

"I'm his mother, Jacob's mother," was all she could say, her voice cracking as she did so.

"Oh, I'm sorry, Mrs. Foley. I didn't recognize you."

She forced a faint smile, suddenly desperate to get out of there.

"I want to help with the search." She heard herself say the opposite.

"Now, ma'am, I do understand but I strongly advise against it. We're covering every inch of the woodland from here down to the coastal road. If your son is out there, we will find him. The best thing you can do now is wait at home. Sheriff Reid will keep you posted."

Out of options, MJ nodded even though she didn't agree. Inside her chest, her emotions were in conflict. On the one hand, she was desperate to do whatever it took to find her son but she was equally desperate to retrieve the parcel she'd hidden in the forest to protect him. Deciding that it was better not to draw any further attention to herself, she thanked him and continued the short distance to her home. But if there was one quality Mary-Jean Foley knew she had, it was perseverance. She'd bide her time and wait till the sun cast shadows between the trees before she went back to recover the parcel. With any luck, they'd miss it, or better still, they'd find Jacob and this would all be over.

When she stepped inside her house, she found Joe waiting for her in the living room, a strange expression on his face.

"What's wrong?" Panic flooded her insides.

"I think it's time we have a talk, MJ."

She popped her handbag on the nearby table.

"I don't have the energy to talk about our marriage, Joe. All I care about is finding Jacob."

"It's not about us, MJ."

She glanced back at him, noticing for the first time her neatly wrapped silk-scarf parcel on the seat next to him.

She drew in a sharp breath and clutched at her pearls.

"Where did you get that?" she asked, trying to mask the nerves.

"Where you buried it, MJ, where else?"

"How did you—?"

"I saw you, MJ, on my way back from dropping Teddy off with Jason and Ann. I thought I'd take a walk back through the forest, just in case I found Jacob hiding out somewhere. Imagine my surprise when I found my wife burying her son's drugs instead! Evidence that the deputies should have found. How could you do this, MJ? Why?"

Her mind ceased working.

"Dare I ask what you were planning on telling them if one of their search-and-rescue dogs uncovered this out there? Do you even realize what you've done?"

Anger bubbled up inside her as Joe continued his rant.

"Your son is clearly in over his head, MJ, and you just made it worse by covering it all up! Have you stopped to think how this affects our standing in church?"

She couldn't hold back any longer.

"Really, Joe? What exactly did you want me to do? Let them find it in his room? Do you honestly think they would have continued looking for Jacob as hard as they are now if they knew he was knee-deep into committing a crime? They would have treated it entirely differently. Treated us differently! And they would arrest him, Joe! Lock him away for the rest of his life."

"Perhaps that should be the consequences he'd have to face for doing crime in the first place."

His words stabbed at her heart.

"That's a horrible thing to say. He's my son, our son, or have you now conveniently chosen to switch out of that role? What's happened to showing people the grace you so often preach about, Joe? Or does your grace not apply to my son?"

She snatched the parcel from the sofa and stuffed it inside her purse.

"You need to turn it over to the sheriff, MJ, or I will wash my hands from having any part in this."

"I will do nothing of the sort, Joe. I will protect my son with everything I have inside me, with or without your help!"

CHAPTER THIRTY

MJ dropped down onto Jacob's bed, tears running uncontrollably down her cheeks. The sting of betrayal over her husband's reaction clung to her heart. Under ordinary circumstances, she would have understood his choice to uphold the law, to do what was right. But this was different. This was family. This was personal. Betrayal turned to bitterness and soon hatred. She would have defended Teddy if it were him instead of Jacob. Why wouldn't he do the same for her son? Why would he choose pride and his reputation over love and grace? Over her and Jacob? Surely, all that mattered most was finding her son.

Time passed quickly while she lay crying on Jacob's bed, her mind swirling with despair, her heart heavy with anguish.

But as was typical of MJ, wallowing in self-pity was

not how she'd dealt with what life had already thrown at her. And when she had no more self-pity left in her, she fell back on the resilience she had always been able to count on when life dealt her a tough hand.

So, she pushed herself off the now-damp pillow and swung her legs over the side of the bed. Wiping her face with her sleeves, she straightened her spine, threw her shoulders back, and took a deep breath to refocus her mind.

Her eyes went to her purse that had dropped onto the floor. Jacob had secrets, that much she already knew. But what if he had hidden more than she'd already found? What if the deputies had missed something? Something that might make sense to her now that didn't before.

Staying seated on the bed, she let her eyes scan the dimly lit room. From the bedside table next to her back to his closet. There had to be something they'd all missed. She chewed at the inside corner of her lip, her mind now thinking like her son's. She thought back to when he was much younger. Recalled habits, little things he used to do. Then it dawned on her. As a child, Jacob kept all his keepsakes inside his Bible. From baseball cards to the letter his dad had left him before he died.

She turned her attention to his bedside table. When his Bible was nowhere to be seen she yanked open the small drawer. This too turned up empty. Now on her knees, she searched on the floor behind it, then under the bed. Nothing. Two strides took her to his desk and she yanked the drawer open. When Jacob's Bible popped into view, she snatched it up and dropped it onto the desk in front of her. Nerves had settled in the pit of her stomach. Whatever she might find would be okay, she told herself. It would never change how much she loved him.

Holding the Bible up, a cover gripped in each hand, she tipped it over, shaking whatever contents were hidden inside to drop onto the desk. When there was nothing else left between the thin pages, her hands searched through the items that had fallen onto the desk. Scripture cards, a few handwritten notes, his dad's letter, and a gold baseball card. Disappointed, MJ dropped the Bible on top of the objects. "Speak to me, Jakey. Help me find you," she whispered as her eyes darted between several trinkets on the nearby shelf. A photo of him and Teddy eating ice cream at the town fair came into view.

Teddy!

She ran out into the hallway and burst into Teddy's room, nearly scaring his headphones off his head while he had been quietly lying in his bed watching a movie on his tablet.

"Sorry, honey, I didn't mean to scare you." She propped herself on the side of his bed and pulled the headset away from his ears.

"Teddy, honey, did Jacob give you anything to keep safe for him? Anything at all? It's very important. It might help us find him."

She waited and studied Teddy's face as he looked at her in quiet contemplation. Then he nodded.

"What, honey, show me!" She tried her best to stay calm but inside her, anxious excitement threatened to explode from every cell.

Teddy hopped out of bed and pulled a tub of ice cream from the cooler under his bed.

"Sweetheart, it's not time for ice cream now. I have to find Jacob."

Teddy's brow furrowed as his head cocked to one side.

"I know, Mama. I am helping you."

The air pushed from inside her lungs as she let out a disappointed sigh. For a brief moment, she thought of leaving, before he wasted any more of her time. But before she could get up, Teddy had already popped the lid off one of the containers and shoved it in her face. A small black mobile phone came into view.

Anxiety pushed into her chest, threatening to erupt from the back of her throat. But she held her excitement back, for fear of Joe interfering and handing it over to Angus.

With the mobile phone in her lap, she pulled Teddy closer, cupping his face in her hands as she tilted his eyes to her.

"You are a hero, Teddy. Thank you. Mama's going to buy you the biggest tub of your favorite ice cream tomorrow, with extra sprinkles."

His eyes lit up, followed by a grin so huge it wrinkled

under her hands. She kissed his forehead and popped the headphones back over his ears before she raced back to Jacob's room.

In the quiet of his room, she sat back on his bed and turned the phone on, suddenly nervous all over again. A hollow feeling nestled in the cavity between her stomach and her heart and she took one deep breath while she watched the phone come to life. She went to the text messages first, searching for the most recent one. It was short, only a brief sentence stating a time and some abbreviations she could not understand.

Her fingers scrolled to the dozen other messages, all written with the same abbreviated words but at different times, noting all of the times were in the early morning hours on different days. A chill ran down her spine. She needed no more convincing. Her son was without a doubt involved in something criminal. Still none the wiser as to where Jacob had met the recipients, she turned her attention to the saved contacts. There were only two numbers saved in the phone's address book. Someone called Dragon and someone who went by the name Moses.

Without a second thought, her thumb scrolled to the one marked as Dragon. She had already pieced it together. She had seen the photo of the dragon tattoo on the McGee boy's chest. Not to mention the significance of the dragon insignia on the ski mask in her purse. Truth suddenly slapped its cold hand across her face. Jacob and Aaron McGee were partners in crime.

Tremors settled into her fingers as her thumb pushed down on the number before she held the phone to her ear. The line clicked off without as much as one ring. Of course, she knew he wouldn't answer. He was, after all, lying on a slab in the morgue. But she was in denial, desperate to have someone answer just to tell her it was all just a horrible nightmare. Panic forced down on her already tight chest and she pushed herself up onto her feet.

"You can do this, MJ. For Jacob," she whispered then drew in several deep breaths before her thumb pressed down on the only other number on the screen: Moses.

CHAPTER THIRTY-ONE

Three short rings and someone on the other end of the line answered her call. Her stomach did a quick flip.

She waited, hearing breathing.

"Jacob, honey, is that you?"

She knew it couldn't be but desperation lay shallow in her heart.

Hope shattered as an unfamiliar man's voice came over the small speaker.

"Your son said you were smart but I'll be honest, Mary Jean, I thought I'd hear from you two days ago."

Fear rippled through her body, her hands gripping the small phone as she pressed it so close to her ear that her pearl stud cut into the soft flesh behind her ear.

"Who is this? Where's Jacob? What have you done with my son?"

Tears sat shallow behind her eyes.

A sadistic laugh left the man's throat.

"He's safe, for now."

"What do you mean for now? Where is he?"

"Where I put people who try to steal from me."

MJ's body went cold, the air in her lungs suddenly trapped.

"If you hurt my son I will—"

"What? Call our little sheriff? Please, spare me, Mary Jean."

She cringed when he said her name.

"What do you want, Moses?"

Two can play this game!

Again he laughed.

"Your son owes me, Mary Jean."

Present tense! He's still alive!

"I'll give it back. Whatever it is I'll give it back to you but please, let my son go!"

"I think you know what it is, Mary Jean. I've had my eye on you."

Another jolt of fear leaped in her stomach. She didn't know what he wanted and the thought of this man watching her every move pushed the sick into her throat. She needed to stay strong. Fake her way through this. Get Jacob back.

"Then you know that I have it and that I'll give it all back. Just tell me where and I'll meet you."

Another sadistic laugh came over the phone.

"You'll give it all back, everything your son owes me?"

"Yes, everything," she lied, her voice dry with deceit as she still had no clue what he was referring to.

"There had better not be one gram or bill missing, Mary Jean."

MJ's head snapped back to her purse. The money!

"I have your money. It's here. Tell me where to meet you and I'll bring it to you. On condition you let my son go."

She bit down on her lip the instant her bargaining words left her mouth.

The man went quiet.

She waited, hearing him breathing.

Had she made a mistake to give him an ultimatum?

"Hello?" she called out with as much confidence as she could fake.

"How do I know you actually have it and that you're not trying to trick me?" he said.

"I'm not! I swear. I found it hidden in his room. It's got red elastic tied around it. The white stuff too."

She had no idea why she told him about the rubber band or the drugs but it had just rolled off her tongue before she could stop herself.

He went quiet.

She waited. Then finally he spoke.

"If I find out you're lying or trying to trick me, or if I as much as see the sheriff's car anywhere, I'll kill your boy. Then I'll come for you."

He's still alive!

"I'm telling you the truth. You have my word. I have your money and your drugs."

Several seconds passed, her heart beating so hard against her chest she was certain he could hear it.

"Take the old coastal road out of town. Turn left where the forest ends. Leave your car in the clearing. Take the path toward the river mouth. I'll be waiting. You have fifteen minutes or your boy is dead."

Energy pushed into her veins as she tucked the man's directions in the back of her mind. This was her chance to find Jacob. To get her son back safely and to bring him home.

"I'll be there. But how do I know you'll stick to your side of the deal?"

His answer was quick.

"I don't play games when it comes to my business, Mary Jean. I have no use for him anymore. But be warned, I don't take kindly to traitors either. Come alone and tell no one or you will never see your boy alive again."

The phone went dead in her ear.

Her body stalled for the briefest of moments before she snapped into action and shoved the phone inside her purse.

When she was halfway to the front door, Joe's voice came from the kitchen.

"You had better be going to see Angus, MJ, or heaven help me I'll go to him myself."

His threatening words sliced deeper into the already open wounds in her heart and she snapped back.

"Not that you care about anyone else except yourself and your precious reputation, Joe, but I am actually going to save my son! Wash your hands all you want but right now I'm doing what I must to get Jacob back home safely."

She was out the door before he could respond and she ran toward her car. Time was against her and saving her son was all she could focus on at that moment.

When MJ slipped behind the wheel and turned her car toward the coastal road at the edge of town, her heart was hard, her mind fixed on her task at hand. With urgency pushing at her from all sides, she drove faster. Jacob was still alive and that's all she cared about. She could do this, with or without anyone's help. It wouldn't be the first time. She had learned a very long time ago that she could only depend on herself. It's what had taught her to fight back, push on, and win, no matter what life threw at her. She didn't need anything from anyone. Not from Joe. Not from Sheriff Angus. Not from God. None of them had shown up for her anyway. All these years she had thrown herself into being the perfect mother, the perfect wife, the perfect Christian. Doing everything her husband and church expected of her. Everything the Bible said she should do. And none of it gave her anything in return when she needed it most.

Anger filled her heart and she turned her voice heavenward.

"Where are you now when I need you most, God? Haven't I done everything you've asked of me? Haven't I proven my commitment to your church?"

But when her angered questions were unanswered with nothing but the humming of her car's engine in her ears, she pushed down even harder on the accelerator.

The clearing stretched out in front of her as her car took the last curve in the sandy road toward the beach. When she got out and took a moment to look around, there was an eerie feeling in the air. As if she was being watched. Perhaps he was watching. Perhaps Moses was perched somewhere to see if she was alone.

Above her head, several seagulls squawked in awkward circles over her head, a last late-night gathering during breeding season before they bedded down and roosted for the night. She ducked when one flew too close to her as if it was warning her to stay away. As if she was trespassing on their territory.

Her eyes found the coastal path and she wasted no time in following it down to the mouth of the river. When she reached the end of the footpath where it stopped at the edge of the marsh she halted. Panic soon made way for doubt. She must have misunderstood his directions, or taken a wrong turn in the dark. There was nothing there, a dead end. She called out to him. Silence returned.

"I'm here. I have your stuff."

But Moses was nowhere to be seen or heard.

She turned around in a small circle and looked back

toward the clearing. Somewhere to her right she heard rustling from between the grassy dunes.

"Hello?" Her voice drifted hollowly into the soft breeze.

"Is anyone there?" she called out again when she was certain she heard someone running away between the dunes.

A dark cloud covered the moon, turning what was somewhat visible into eerie shadows that made it even harder to see between the grassy dunes behind her. When her nerves were at their peak, she turned back around and stared between the dense shrubs that were at the end of the footpath, squinting into the darkness.

Then she saw it. A small, faint light gently swayed high above the water. Realizing it was a boat, she pulled the foliage away. Tucked between the dense foliage and tall reeds a houseboat quietly bopped in the small, choppy ripples of the river mouth.

CHAPTER THIRTY-TWO

As evening set in, soon to cover the town's secrets and lies in a cloak of darkness, Angus set off toward the marina. Determined not to let evil prevail, he pulled his car into a concealed spot at the far side of the pier. From his position, he had a clear view of the main docking bays and the manager's office, even in the pale light where the sun dipped behind the horizon.

With his vehicle's engine and lights switched off, he lifted a pair of binoculars to his face, setting his sights on the faint light that beamed from inside the office. As he waited for the stocky manager to make his move, he panned his view across the marina, seizing the opportunity to look for the boat with blue paint. But for the most part, the docks were occupied by small private sailboats and a few local fishing trawlers, none of which had any semblance of blue paint visible from what he could see.

Time dragged by as Angus waited and watched the manager's every move. He had popped in and out between boats a few times, but nothing that warranted suspicion.

At times Angus contemplated abandoning his stakeout, reasoning that his help might be much more needed alongside his search team. He was after all acting on a hunch.

But no matter how many times he got ready to leave, he couldn't. As if something, or someone, nudged him to stay put, to wait, to be patient.

Dark clouds threatened to conceal whatever secrets were locked away in Weyport but his eyes remained fixed on the manager's office. Throughout the evening, the dim light in his office never switched off once nor did the stocky manager move from his chair for several hours. As if he too was waiting for something.

With his instincts and hopes high, Angus stayed put, only every so often shuffling in his seat to shift the discomfort in his body. Nearly two hours into his stakeout, his eyes caught a small light in the distance across the ocean. His spine straightened almost instantly and he aimed his binoculars at it. The light grew brighter as the boat neared the marina entrance and suddenly every cell in his body was on high alert. This was it, the moment he'd been waiting for. He could feel it. Excitement rushed through his limbs, his sights never once leaving the boat as it eventually slowed into a docking space. Desperate to find out if Jacob was in the boat, Angus slipped out of his car and stealthily made his way toward it. Several yards from its dock, the overhead light of the mooring illuminated the entire port side of the unremarkable boat. As he traced the name on the side of the boat, his breath caught in his throat.

Mermaid's Tail. It was one of the names on the cork-board. He clocked the time on his watch, again comparing it to his recall of the clandestine manifest on the cork-board. It matched.

Hiding behind a stack of empty fishing crates in an adjacent dock, Angus watched as two men jumped out onto the quay to moor the boat. Guns glistened on their hips in the pale light. He pointed his binoculars at their faces, instantly recognizing one of them from the day he saw Jacob at the skate park.

His heart skipped a beat. This was enough proof that the two cases were linked. Aaron and Jacob were more than just commuters on a school bus. They were working together. And by the looks of things, working for some seriously bad people.

But as quickly as his heart beat with elation over being one step closer to solving their cases, it dropped into the pit of his stomach. Because at that moment, Angus realized that the odds of finding Jacob alive grew slimmer by the second and that it would take nothing short of a miracle to prevent him from suffering the same fate as Aaron McGee.

Tension soaked into every fiber of his body as Angus

kept his eyes on the duo of armed men waiting on the dock.

Then, from inside the office, the stocky manager's frame suddenly burst through the doorway and rushed toward the two men, straining with the weight of two large duffle bags he carried in each hand. When he met up with the two men there was a quick muted conversation before the manager handed over a bag to each of the men. After briefly checking the contents of their bags, the guy from the skate park pulled out two thick wads of cash and gave it to the manager, leaving a fat grin on his bearded face. Without any further exchange, the armed men boarded the motorboat and, with the same stealth as they had arrived, motored their way back out to sea.

Angus dropped down behind the crates, elated and shocked at the same time with the payoff he had just witnessed. In his experience money exchanges like this one reeked of only two things: drug trafficking or money laundering, and in most cases, the two options were almost always linked.

But going in guns blazing without backup would only harm his chances of ever finding Jacob. He had to be smart, wait for the right time to strike, and trust that it wouldn't be too late.

The night air was cold and damp against his skin where he sat hiding behind the crates. If his suspicions were correct, the second boat would be pulling up into the dock shortly. Deciding to wait it out, Angus settled in behind the crates, one eye on the manager who had disappeared back inside his office.

Forty-five minutes later, the second boat turned up, its name and timeline once again matching the corkboard manifest. Relying on his experience, Angus took out his smartphone and aimed his video recorder directly at them. As with the earlier routine, the manager repeated the delivery, this time, handing over just one bag but again receiving a handsome payout in exchange.

When the second boat had left and the stocky manager had returned to his office, Angus took his moment.

Caught off guard, the stubby marina manager nearly had a heart attack as he sat counting out the cash at his desk when Angus exploded through his door.

"Get your hands up!" Angus yelled at him, his Glock 22 pointed directly at his chest.

"Take it easy, Sheriff!" he said, his hands now up over his head.

"Step away from your desk, slowly."

The manager didn't react.

"I said, step away from your desk and put your hands behind your head."

The manager raised his hands as he shuffled his thickset body away from his desk to do as he was told.

Angus approached him with caution, his gun aimed firmly at the center of his chest.

"Turn around, nice and steady."

"Come now, Sheriff. I'm sure we can sort something out here."

"I said turn around, slowly," Angus repeated, his knuckles white as he gripped his weapon.

"You don't have to do this, you know, Sheriff." The manager persisted while he turned his back on Angus. "I told you, in this town we take care of each other. And trust me, I can take care of you if you let me. I rub your back you rub mine, you know? I mean, let's face it, they're not paying you a fortune here. I'm sure you can do with the odd bonus or two, right."

CHAPTER THIRTY-THREE

Angus ignored him and with the manager's back now turned toward Angus, he holstered his gun before he cuffed the manager's arms behind his back.

"Sit down," Angus said, as he spun him back around to face him, then nudged him down in his chair.

"Where's the boy?"

A smirk broke on the manager's face.

"Which boy?"

Angus wasn't about to let the man toy with him so he pushed the cash on the desk around with the tip of his gun.

"There's quite a lot of money here. Suppose I arrest you and put the word out that you held back more than you were supposed to from those bags you handed over earlier. What do you think might happen to you then?"

He watched the manager's stunned face.

"You're bluffing. Besides, since when is it a crime to have cash in my office?" He pivoted. "A lot of my private boats pay cash to moor their boats. You've got nothing on me, Sheriff."

Angus smiled and pulled his phone from his pocket.

"I'd think twice about that if I were you. You never know what people see when they stare out at the ocean."

The stubby manager squirmed in his chair, his eyes riddled with questions while he watched Angus slide his thumb over his mobile.

"So, let me ask you again. Where's the boy?" This time Angus's voice was heavy with warning, his eyes grim as he looked the manager straight in the eye.

"Like I said, Sheriff, I have no idea what you're talking about. Now, if you're going to arrest me for counting my revenue, then do so. If not, take these cuffs off me before you—"

"Before I what? End up dead in the marsh like the McGee boy?"

The manager turned his face away.

"Let's quit playing games, shall we?" Angus said as he flipped his phone around and shoved the screen closer to the guy's face.

The manager turned white as he watched the video footage of his earlier transaction in the dock play out. When the clip ended, Angus locked eyes with him again.

"Where's the Foley boy? Tell me or I release this clip

to everyone who has their noses stuck in their smart-phones. My guess is you'll be found dead in the marshes before the sun sets tomorrow."

The manager sucked back on his teeth and looked away.

"I don't know anything about a Foley boy. That's the truth. And what happened to the kid whose body was found in the salt marsh had nothing to do with me. I do what I'm told and that's it. I can't help it if he tried to steal from him."

Angus's gaze lingered on the man's face, his eyes searching for the truth.

"Let's say I believe you. How about you give me your best guess about who you think did have something to do with his death?"

Again, the manager looked away, his demeanor even more reluctant than before.

"If I tell you, I'm as dead as the McGee kid, with or without you sharing that video clip."

"Well then, from where I'm sitting you're in a tough spot. At least if you tell me, you'll have a better chance of surviving since you'll be safely tucked away in a county jail cell. On the other hand, I can leak this video and keep you cuffed to your desk where he will find you. What he does with you then is up to him."

"You can't be serious! Aren't you supposed to serve and protect your town?"

"I don't protect nor serve criminals. Now get on with it

and tell me where to start looking for the missing boy. I'll make it really easy for you. If I'm right, and I think I am, whoever you're working for owns a boat. A blue one, to be precise."

Surprise flashed across the man's face, contemplation clearly in his eyes. A few moments later, his body slumped in defeat.

"There's a dirt road that turns off the coastal road, down where the forest ends. On the other end of the clearing, a footpath will take you between the dunes to a small inlet near the mouth of the river."

Angus didn't waste a moment more and slipped in behind the manager to shackle his hands to his chair instead.

"Hey! You said you were going to protect me! I gave you what you wanted; now either let me go or take me to jail. You can't leave me here like this! They'll kill me!"

But Angus was already in the doorway, his fingers moving over the lock in the door as he replied, "Oh, I can. But don't worry, I'll be back to tuck you into your jail cot myself before you know it. Unless they get to you first, of course. So sit tight, and don't miss me too much." He winked at the manager as he said it then turned and left, locking the door behind him.

"Very funny!" the manager yelled after him. "My blood will be on your hands, Sheriff! Explain that to the folk in your new town! You're done for!"

But Angus was already halfway to his car, ignoring the idle threats that continued to be thrown at him from inside the closed office. He'd deal with the guy later; after he rescued Jacob.

CHAPTER THIRTY-FOUR

Angus followed the tree line along the old coastal road to where it eventually stopped. On the opposite side of the forest, the sandy road was exactly where the marina manager had said it would be. He pulled over onto the shoulder and rested for a minute.

The area was quiet, almost forbidding. From where he sat in his Durango asking for courage and strength, he could see his search-and-rescue team's flashlights beaming in the distance through the dense forestry to his right. At first, he thought of calling in for backup but then decided his men were more needed in the forest search. He'd play it extra safe, watch his back, and stay alert.

With his mind set on finding Jacob, he checked the rounds in his Glock's magazine before he holstered his gun again, leaving the clasp of the holster undone.

With his headlights off, he turned down onto the

sandy road, his eyes searching out danger, his body vigilant. When he reached the end of the road where it opened up to the clearing, he saw the outlines of a parked vehicle in the faint moonlight. Slowing down, he drove toward it. As he got closer, the outlines took on more definition and the wood-paneled sides of a light brown Dodge Caravan came into full view.

His heart caught in his chest as he instantly recognized the vehicle. He knew of only one person in town who owned a car like that. And she had every reason to want to be there.

A restless feeling came over him as he stopped his vehicle across from MJ's car, turning on his headlights to illuminate it. His eyes darted between the seats as he searched for her inside. When he couldn't see her, he drove a circle around her vehicle and parked slightly behind it. With one hand now on his holstered gun and the other shining his flashlight out in front of him, he stepped out of his vehicle and approached her car with caution, peering in on all sides as he circled it. Satisfied the car was empty he shone his light across the clearing and into the nearby grassy dunes. When he caught sight of the footpath the manager told him to take, he set off toward it.

The soft sand pushed away beneath his feet as he wound his way along the path toward the mouth of the river. Sensing danger in the quiet darkness around him, he pulled his gun and tucked it under his flashlight hand.

Once he got to the end of the footpath, the light fell onto the shadows of a houseboat.

He held back, scouted the area, and listened for sounds.

Silence.

Then a woman's chilling scream pierced the darkness.

MJ!

Angus charged toward the boat, every part of his body tense and on high alert, his gun pointed out in front of him. Around him, everything went quiet. Too quiet.

When he got close to the boat, he stopped, his eyes scanning the perimeter. Adrenaline surged through his veins, his palm pressing firmly against his gun's grip.

Directly ahead of him, the boat bobbed peacefully in the water, as if the scream he heard wasn't real. As if nothing had disturbed the surrounding tranquility.

But he knew what he had heard. There was no mistaking the shrill sound that still echoed in his mind.

Certain it came from the boat, he moved closer, looking over his shoulders as he got next to the small vessel.

As he stepped onto the boat, dread suddenly filled his heart. Visions of finding both MJ and Jacob dead inside the boat flooded his mind. He pushed them aside. Shot up a prayer. Forced the evil from his heart and mind.

God was with him, with them, protecting them from evil.

Taking note of the weathered royal blue paint on the

deck floor, illuminated only by the dim flickering overhead light, he walked toward the narrow entrance. Several boards creaked beneath his feet as he inched toward the door that stood ajar, warning him to be extra careful. He switched his flashlight off, tucking it under his weapon with two fingers. But instinct told him to rest his thumb on the small button just in case. With both hands on his gun, aimed at the dark space beyond the door, he entered the belly of the boat. Inch by inch he moved through the dark space.

A slight shuffle came toward him from the far side. Adrenaline whirled inside his stomach. He stopped and fell back behind the doorpost, his fingers gripped so tight around his pistol that the steel handle dented the soft flesh of his palms.

He listened.

Took a deep breath.

Decided to proceed.

With his senses heightened, his eyes piercing through the shadowy space, his thumb found the small button of his flashlight.

In one swift move, he shone the flashlight toward the shuffling noise, his firearm pointed directly into the beam of light.

Then he saw her, slumped down against the wall on the far side, her face and clothing covered in blood, her eyes staring directly at him.

Tension ripped through his body like an electric shock,

his feet ready to rush toward her, his instincts telling him to act with caution.

He shifted his flashlight in all directions and surveyed the rest of the room with deliberate swift movements. When it appeared they were alone he rushed to her side.

"MJ, it's me, Angus. Are you hurt?"

He shone his flashlight just below her chin, lighting up her entire face. Streaks of black makeup ran trails down her damp cheeks. She just sat there, staring out in front of her without uttering a word. Angus gently touched her cheek, in that instant thinking that she was no longer alive, but her eyes glimmered for the briefest of moments before her gaze met his.

"It's going to be okay, MJ. Are you hurt?" He tried again. This time she shook her head ever so slightly.

"Good, that's great to hear. Can you tell me what happened?"

But MJ's eyes watered up, the rest of her body remaining slumped without any motion as her hands rested lifelessly on the floor next to her.

"MJ, where's Jacob? Did you come here to find him?"

Tears ran freely down her face, her eyes filled with so much sorrow Angus feared the worst for Jacob.

Deciding he wasn't getting anywhere with her in the state she was in, he panned his flashlight down toward the floor beneath her extended legs. A trail of fresh blood stained the floor beside her and he followed it with his flashlight to where it ended in a large pool of blood a few feet away.

When his flashlight searched the space next to it, he saw the body, lying flat on the floor a gaping bullet hole in the middle of his chest.

CHAPTER THIRTY-FIVE

Reflexes took over and Angus was up on his feet, his flashlight positioned under his weapon in front of him as he searched for the killer. On the far end wall, he darted toward the light switch, flicking it on as he remained on guard. When the entire room lit up he noticed the table formation; little stations lining the walls as if products were on display at a church fete.

When he was sure no one else was in the room with them, he rushed over to the body and pressed two fingers on his neck.

His eyes scanned the man's face. Using his flashlight, Angus lifted the red-tinted Aviators that were already half off his face to fully expose his eyes. There was no denying it. The man was dead.

Back at MJ's side, Angus holstered his firearm and squeezed her shoulder.

"It's going to be okay, MJ, but you need to tell me what happened. Where's Jacob? Have you seen him?"

Fresh tears dropped onto her chin, her eyes finally responding to his questions as she shook her head and spoke for the first time.

"He's gone. My boy is gone." Her shoulders shook uncontrollably as her stupor turned into a fresh wave of sobbing.

"He's not gone, MJ. I will not accept that. We have to find him. Tell me what happened."

His voice was urgent, his heart heavy.

She shrugged her shoulders.

"I don't know where he is. I'll never know where he is. Moses was supposed to give him back. Now he's dead and took my baby boy with him to the grave." A whining sound left her throat anew.

Angus looked back at the frizzy-haired man on the floor.

"That's Moses?"

MJ nodded.

"Did you kill him?" He forced the question.

Her eyes shot an accusing look his way.

"Sorry, I had to ask. Did you see who did?"

MJ shook her head.

"Was he dead when you got here then?"

She nodded.

"Did you see or hear anyone else?"

"No," she said as her chin dropped to her chest.

"Are you sure, MJ? It's very important. Even the smallest detail might help us find Jacob. Think carefully. Did you hear or see anything else?"

After a small pause, MJ responded, her eyes suddenly bright.

"Between the dunes. I heard something. It sounded like someone was running away. I thought it was Jacob."

Hope turned to despair once more.

"We'll find him, MJ, don't lose faith, okay? We will find Jacob!"

Angus was already on his mobile phone reporting the incident along with a request for medical assistance. Next, he called Miguel to move the K-9 search-and-rescue unit from the forest to his location.

He turned his attention back to the bloody scene to his side. There were no signs of struggle, evident by the table and chairs that were undisturbed directly behind Moses. The lenses of his sunglasses were also still intact nor did he have any lesions on his face or hands. Next, he searched the room for the murder weapon. Judging by the gaping wound in Moses' chest Angus guessed it to be a shotgun, fired at close range.

His gaze settled upon the door and he walked over to it. The latch was partially unhinged. He shone his flash-light onto the doorpost. The wood was splintered, confirming his suspicion that the door was kicked in. With no murder weapon in sight, he turned his attention back to MJ where she still sat quietly on the other side of the room. His gut told him she couldn't have killed Moses. She simply didn't have the strength or skill to break through the door. And since Jacob was still missing, she had no motive to kill him either.

When he reached her, he lifted her off the floor. She was in shock and it was evident that he wasn't going to get any more answers out of her as long as she was in her current state. And staring at the bloody body on the floor only made it worse.

"Let's get some fresh air, MJ."

She let him help her out onto the deck where he had her away from the scene of the crime and looking out across the water instead. The moon danced atop the small ripples as it stretched its glow out along the river. He let his eyes trail the grassy banks, his faith and hope pinned on finding Jacob before it was too late.

Soon after, Angus heard the approaching sirens in the distance and he silently pleaded that they hurried up. Time was of the essence and finding Jacob was all he could focus on right now. Catching the killer was of secondary concern.

The gentle breeze was cool and seemed to help MJ come out of her stupor so when he noticed that she was more attentive to her surroundings he seized the moment. This time his voice was more composed.

"MJ, why were you here? Tell me what happened so I can find your son. He needs you now more than ever, MJ. Help me find Jacob."

Her eyes met his and for a brief moment, Angus thought she was going to cry again. But she didn't. Instead, he saw strength behind her demeanor. Courage even. Her hand slipped inside her purse that was still draped across her body. When she pulled it out she clutched a disposable phone in her hand and held it out to him.

"I found this at home. It's Jacob's. The McGee boy's number is on it along with one other."

"Moses." Angus finished her sentence.

She nodded.

"So you called the guy."

Again, she nodded then stuck her hand back inside her purse to pull out the wad of cash and sachets of white powder.

Shame fell upon her face when Angus took it from her.

"I'm not judging, MJ, it's okay."

A lonely tear rolled down her cheek as MJ continued.

"I found this in Jacob's room, the day the deputies were there to search it. I hid it in the forest. I was only trying to protect Jacob, I swear."

"Go on."

"When I called Moses he told me to meet him here and to give him back what Jacob stole from him. I assumed he was talking about this so I told him I had it but that I'd only give it to him if he let Jacob go. But when I got here he was lying on the floor, barely breathing." MJ started to sob again. "I tried to keep him alive so he could tell me where Jacob was. I tried everything. Nothing worked. The blood was everywhere and I couldn't understand him with all the blood in his mouth. Now he's dead and Jacob—"

"I'll find him, MJ, I promise you. If it's the last thing I do, I will find Jacob."

She nodded through a fresh wave of gentle tears.

"MJ, I need you to think back to when you found Moses. What did he say? Think carefully, MJ. Could you make out anything he said? Anything at all."

MJ drew in a few sharp breaths as she tried to calm her soft sobs.

"I can't be sure but he said something about a bear. But it doesn't make any sense. We don't find black bears this far south so I think I must have heard wrong."

CHAPTER THIRTY-SIX

B ehind them, panting dogs dragged their handlers toward the boat as the K-9 unit was first to arrive at the scene, shortly followed by two medics and Miguel.

"They're going to take good care of you, MJ. I'll find Jacob, okay? Go with them and I'll call you as soon as I know anything."

"No! I'm coming with you. I'm not going to wait around anymore, Angus. They've been out there searching for days now and no one has come any closer to finding my son. I found this place. I found Moses. I will find Jacob too!"

Angus wanted to say no, wanting to follow procedure. But having seen the strength in her eyes mere moments ago, and now noticing the desperation in her eyes, he simply didn't have the heart to deny her the hope of finding her son.

"Are you sure about this, MJ? There's no telling what we might find." He chose his words carefully.

She nodded without blinking, her shoulders back and fortitude emanating from her core.

"Fine, but stay close and stay between Miguel and me. There's always a chance that the killer might still be around here somewhere."

Again, MJ agreed, wiping the final remnants of tears from her face with a blood-free spot on her sleeve.

A quick briefing to the K-9 unit had them deploy the dogs in the opposite direction along the coastline and between the nearby sand dunes while the rest of his team set about blocking off and working the immediate scene around the boat.

Angus turned his attention to Miguel.

"MJ said this guy mumbled something about a bear before he died. You grew up in Weyport. Any idea what he might have been talking about?"

Miguel furrowed his brow and shook his head.

"Not a clue, Sheriff, sorry. I've never heard of anyone seeing any bears out here and I'd say the chances of finding any are extremely slim." He paused then looked up. "Except there used to be a few old culverts farther up the river. As kids, people used to tell us bears hid out in them; obviously, so we didn't go near them. But when the river flooded nearly ten years ago, they decided to divert the stormwater into the reservoir instead. The culverts have been entirely inaccessible since then."

"A couple of remote stormwater drains sound like a good place to start. Let's work our way up from here along the river. Think you can find them?"

"Absolutely. I know this area like the back of my hand. We used to come here all the time as kids. There's a fishing spot not far from here and the culverts are just a bit north of there."

Their game plan was interrupted when a female voice sounded directly behind Angus. It was Murphy.

"What do you have for me, Sheriff?" Her face had lost its previous amiable features and carried in its stead a far grimmer guise.

"Thanks for getting here so quickly, Murphy. Our victim is in there." Angus pointed toward the boat behind him. "Gunshot wound to the chest. He was still alive when Mrs. Foley found him but bled out before she could get help. As it turns out, our victim appears to also be responsible for our still missing teen."

Murphy turned to MJ, her eyes suddenly full of compassion before she turned her gaze back to Angus.

"You haven't found him yet?" Murphy asked.

"Not yet, which is where you come in," Angus hinted.

"Got it. I have a mobile forensic test unit in my vehicle. It's pretty comprehensive but I might have to call in a few favors if I get stuck. I'll grab as much as I can off him and let you know if there's anything that might help you find the boy, or the killer, of course."

She turned to face MJ.

"I pray God gives you strength, Mrs. Foley. Hang in there."

And with that, she turned and brushed past them onto the boat, leaving Angus to ponder her declaration of faith that completely took him by surprise.

It was Miguel that brought him back to the task at hand when he handed them each a stronger flashlight.

"It's this way," Miguel directed as he shone his flashlight out into the darkness along a mostly overgrown path along the river.

"Let's get on with it then. We don't know how much time we have," Angus prompted before he nodded at Miguel to take the lead.

The three of them set off into the dark night, weaving their way between the dense watery shrubs. With their flashlights beaming out in front of them, they searched for anything that might point them to where Jacob could be. But less than fifteen minutes into their search, MJ suddenly stopped, her shoulders slumped forward as if she was ready to collapse on the spot.

"What if we never find him? What if Moses had already killed him and tricked me into bringing him his money?"

Angus squared himself in front of her.

"You need to keep the faith, MJ. You can't allow yourself to let doubt get the better of you. I gave you my word. We will keep searching for Jacob until we find him."

MJ said what he couldn't say out loud.

"Dead or alive, right, Angus?" Her voice cracked as she said it.

"I choose to believe that God brought us this far for a reason, MJ," Angus said. "Jacob needs us. We now know that he and Aaron McGee worked together. We also know that the McGee boy was killed on Moses' houseboat. The fact that Jacob's body wasn't found on the boat tells me there's a strong possibility that he might still be alive. After all, Moses needed to get his money back first, right?"

MJ nodded, her eyes suddenly alive again.

"What? Do you recall anything?" Angus immediately prompted.

"I'm not sure but you might be right. When I called Moses earlier, from the mobile phone I found in Jacob's shoe, he said he'd expected my call two days ago. The way he spoke gave me the impression that Jacob was still alive."

Hope settled on her face, a fresh surge of energy now pushing through her body.

"We have to keep looking. He has to be around here somewhere. My boy has to be alive."

Her voice was full of conviction, which brought a smile to Angus's face.

"Miguel, you heard her, let's pick up the pace."

The deputy did as he was told and before long they reached the small fishing spot he had mentioned they frequented as children.

"The first drain is up there, just beyond those rocks over there." He pointed up the small embankment where a

URCELIA TEIXEIRA

few sharp boulders laced the river walls. "It's the biggest one of the two. The other drain is about fifty yards farther down the river."

As the trio shone their flashlights out to where Miguel was pointing, MJ drew in a sudden sharp breath as she stared at a spot made brighter by her flashlight.

CHAPTER THIRTY-SEVEN

Angus whipped around, noticing the series of mixed emotions on her face.

"What's wrong?" he asked MJ.

Trepidation ever so slightly concealed her excitement when she answered him.

"I think I see something."

Miguel rushed toward the spot she pointed out, traversing the dense foliage and rocky terrain with hardly any effort. When he got to the place, he yelled back to MJ and Angus.

"It's a sneaker!"

MJ's heart caught in her throat, confusing emotions propelling her to plow through the thick vegetation and over the sharp rocks without a care about the scrapes left in their wake. When she and Angus met up with Miguel, there was not a single doubt in her mind.

"It's his. It's Jacob's sneaker." She clasped both hands in front of her mouth as fear overwhelmed her senses.

"You're absolutely sure?" Angus checked.

She nodded.

"One hundred percent, he wore these sneakers all the time and I remember thinking he must have worn them the day he went missing because they weren't in his closet when I found the money. He loved these shoes."

"Then we're on the right track. Keep your eyes open and watch your backs. Moses might have had a watchman."

Angus had already unclipped his holster and had his hand ready on his firearm. Miguel did the same as he led the small party toward the first culvert.

Apart from the gentle rippling of the river behind them, there wasn't a sound in the cool air around them and they slowly climbed the rocky embankment. MJ's foot caught between two rocks and she squealed with pain as she fell.

Angus rushed to her side.

"Are you hurt?"

"I'm fine, keep going," she lied, aware of the gash across the palm of her hand where the boulder sliced into it when she tried to stop her fall. But she pressed down on it with the bottom of her sleeve, trying her best to hide it from Angus's inquiring eyes.

"You sure you're okay to walk?" he asked once more as

he helped her to her feet, choosing to look beyond the deliberate concealment of the cut on her hand.

"Yes, I'm fine. We need to keep moving. I just want to find my boy."

She was right, he felt it too. They were so close to finding Jacob.

Up on her feet again, MJ pushed on ahead of him until she was only a few steps behind Miguel.

At some point they let Angus take over the lead and when they eventually got close to the water duct, Angus held up one arm, signaling them to stop.

With their flashlights now off and frozen in place outside the mouth of the water conduit, Angus took a moment to scout out their surroundings, battling the flicker of doubt that now threatened to cloud his faith. Experience had taught him that, by now, too much time had already passed and there was a stronger likelihood of finding Jacob dead than alive.

He sent up a quick plea for help, courage, safety, and for God to intervene in the situation against worldly odds.

"I'm going in," MJ suddenly announced when she spotted the hesitation on his face and set off toward the large circular opening.

"MJ, wait! It could be dangerous," Angus warned.

"No, I'm not waiting any longer, Angus. If Jacob is in there we need to get him out. He needs me and every second we waste hanging around here could be a second closer to his death! I'm not waiting. I'm going in."

Angus clenched down on his jaw. She was stubborn but she couldn't have been more right. If Jacob had been held captive in the stormwater pipe all this time he'd be barely alive. He thought of his own longing. If it had been him so close to finding his brother he'd be rushing in there too.

"Fine, but we need to be extra careful. Stay behind me and watch your step."

They fell into formation. Angus in front, then MJ, and finally Miguel. Weapons in hand, senses heightened they slowly approached the cavity. When they got to the round pipe opening, they paused, Miguel on one side, Angus and MJ on the other.

With their flashlights off it was harder to see clearly, made worse by the dark clouds that hung low across the sky. Until the moon peeped out from behind an ominous cloud and shone a faint light directly at the opening as if a divine hand had shone a flashlight down onto the opening. A rusty but solid metal grid that spanned the entire opening came into full view and had on one side a giant padlock and thick chain wrapping its evil claws around it.

"Now what?" MJ whispered, worry all over her face once again.

Miguel's eyes had questions too.

"Stand back," Angus whispered to MJ while his eyes told Miguel to be ready with his weapon.

Miguel's hands wrapped tighter around his pistol, his feet spread apart as much as the rocky terrain would allow.

Angus aimed his firearm directly at the large padlock and pulled back on the trigger.

Clapping sounds echoed between the rocks as the bullet exploded into the padlock, springing it open.

Miguel's flashlight searched the area around them.

"Clear," he announced.

"Stay here," Angus told MJ who right away denied the instruction with her raised eyebrows.

Choosing not to fight her, Angus turned his attention back to the thick chain, working quickly to unwrap it.

When the chain soon fell to the ground, he took up position, flashlight under his weapon stretched out in front of him.

Dirt and smaller pebbles crunched under his feet as he hunched into the opening, the light of his flashlight piercing the pitch-black darkness. Behind him, Miguel mirrored his stance while MJ followed at the back.

Damp, earthy air settled in their nostrils. The deeper they went into the tunnel the colder it got, the icy temperature slicing through their clothes.

From somewhere ahead of them a faint whimpering drifted toward them.

Angus heard it first and stopped to listen more closely.

Again, the whimpering echoed through the underground tunnel.

When this time MJ heard it too she pushed Miguel out of the way and grabbed onto Angus's arm, her grip telling him what he had already suspected.

"It's him, it's my boy," she said, her voice thick with emotion.

MJ pushed past Angus and rushed off into the darkness, her heart pulling at the familiar cry for help like a lioness running to her lost cub.

Guided only by her heart and the urge to find her son she called out into the near darkness.

"Mama's coming, Jakey, hang on, I'm coming!"

From behind, Angus's flashlight cast soft shadows her way, lighting only the walls around her as her body blocked the view in front of her.

The whimpering grew louder.

MJ moved faster.

Then she saw him, his skinny body in a small heap in front of another metal gate.

When Angus shone his flashlight onto Jacob, his swollen eyes stared back at them under the sharp light, his scrawny body looking fragile as he lay on his side, his knees drawn into his chest.

"Jacob!" MJ yelled and fell down beside him.

"I'm here, baby, Mama's here. I got you, my boy, I got you," she said as she pulled her son into her arms.

Jacob's body shivered under her embrace and she pulled him closer, the strong scent of urine hitting her senses.

"Hang on, my boy, we're going to get you out of here, okay? Mama's here, my boy, Mama's here. It's all over now."

Barely able to raise his head, Jacob looked into his mother's face, his once bright hazel eyes now dull and strained with suffering.

"I asked Jesus to help you find me, Mama, and He did. He forgave me and brought you straight to me."

MJ's heart leaped inside her chest as she listened to her son's confession, her mind instantly transported to the time she cuddled him just after his father had died. He was suddenly back there, that young toddler, vulnerable and gullible, with the faith only an innocent child could have.

"Jesus was here with me, Mama. The whole time, He was here with me."

Guilt entered her heart as his words touched the very nerves of her soul. As if she'd been shaken from the inside out. She hung her head, instantly aware of a fresh sin she didn't realize she'd committed until that very moment. Never once had she turned to God for help, held the faith like her young son had, and asked that He would protect her son and bring him home. Instead, she had tried to find Jacob in her own strength, went out, and searched for him herself. There had been too many times she shunned Him, and pushed Jesus aside in anger and frustration instead of hope.

Then it hit her. She, Mary Jean Foley, only called on God when everyone was watching. When she needed to pretend that she had a relationship with Him and that her spirit was whole. But in truth, she had been holding onto anger ever since Jacob's father had died. As if God was the keeper of disease instead of Satan. As if God was to blame.

She was like the Samaritan woman at the well, owning her shame, living her days in death instead of freedom. All this time she had been spiritually thirsty, desperate for an intimate relationship with God. She couldn't trust Him because she didn't know Him, because she hadn't been drinking from His spiritual well of living water. She had been living a life of spiritual bankruptcy. A life riddled with falsehood and sin.

And as she gazed down into her son's eyes that were suddenly filled with wisdom, she silently offered her shame to Jesus and asked Him to transform her heart, to fill her with His Spirit anew, to restore her marriage to Joe, and to give her effervescent life worthy of His praise instead.

CHAPTER THIRTY-EIGHT

Angus shut the door of the ambulance before it drove away with MJ and Jacob inside.

"I've got to give it to you, Sheriff, I didn't think we'd find the boy alive," Miguel said.

"Agreed. I'll admit, I had my moments of doubt too. But God works in mysterious ways, Miguel, and clearly, He had His hand over the Foleys. I just wish we could say the same about the McGee boy."

"What do you make of our victim in there? Think he got what he deserved?"

"No one deserves to be dealt the hand of death by man, Miguel. But since you bring him up, as much as we would like to walk away from all of this, we still have to do our jobs and catch the guy who did this."

"Any idea who might want to kill the guy, Sheriff?" Miguel asked.

"A guy doing what he did? Could be anyone who did business with him."

Angus turned and faced the boat where his team was still working the scene. To one side his K-9 team leader stood with a few of his search-and-rescue members and he walked over.

"Anything for me yet?" Angus enquired.

"I'm afraid not, Sheriff. We picked up a strong scent along the beach but the dogs lost it at the water's edge. It doesn't help that the tide's coming in either."

"Okay, thanks, keep at it and let me know if you find anything new, please."

"Copy that, Sheriff."

Moments later one of his deputies came running over.

"The ME needs you in the boat, Sheriff. She thinks she might have found something."

Elation ripped through Angus's body as he turned and boarded the boat.

"Ah, there you are, Sheriff," Murphy exclaimed when he walked over to where she was still busy examining Moses' body.

"I hear you might have found something," Angus said.

"And I hear you found the Foley boy. I have to say, I was expecting you to hand me a second case tonight." She pulled off her gloves and stood up to face him.

"Me and you both, Murphy, but I can't take all the credit. It was nothing short of a miracle if you ask me.

Now, if only I can catch me a killer tonight, I'd be a happy man."

"Well, I think I might be able to help with that."

She turned and took out a grip seal bag containing a vial from her bag on the table behind her and held it out to Angus.

"What's this?"

"This, dear Sheriff, is traces of an extremely rare Scotch found on the victim's clothing and face."

"So he had expensive taste in his liquor."

"Perhaps, except, he wasn't the one who did the drinking tonight. I did a preliminary DNA test to see if the saliva samples on his face matched his DNA and they didn't. Nor did an oral swab show any signs of alcohol of any kind in his mouth or throat."

"You're confusing me, Murphy. Are you saying he didn't consume any alcohol?"

"Not a single drop as far as I can tell. Of course, I'll know for sure once I cut him open and inspect his stomach contents but since your team couldn't find any liquor on the boat, I'm fairly certain these droplets had been transferred onto him. Most likely by someone who had been doing a lot of drinking and stood close enough to him to eject his saliva onto his clothing and face. In fact, I'd go as far as to say that it is highly likely that it's certain someone spat in our victim's face."

"Someone like our killer," Angus said as he rolled the

sealed bag with the vial between his fingers and mulled over the information he had just learned.

"Could be, yes. I'll have to run the specimens through our database to hopefully find you a name but, unfortunately, I can't do that from out here."

Angus handed the vial back to her.

"You said it's an extremely rare bottle of whiskey. Any idea which one?"

"That I can confirm. Rare and expensive," she announced as she signaled for Angus to follow her to a table that stood to one side where her computer and mobile lab sat on top. "Luckily my friend is working the nightshift up in New York so I had to call in a quick favor." Her fingers clicked a few keys on her laptop before she turned the screen for Angus to see.

When the image of the brand's label came into view, Angus dropped his head in disbelief, his heart suddenly heavy with compassion.

"I see you are familiar with it then," Murphy commented as Angus turned away, his hands now on his hips and his face heavenward.

"This is one of those times I wish that I was wrong. But unfortunately, I saw one of these bottles only a few days ago. And sadly, the man who offered me a glass most definitely had a motive to want to kill our friend over here."

"Oh, one more thing, Sheriff. Just looking at the obvious blue color of the boat, it's fair to say this was where the McGee boy was killed. I've taken a sample of the paint to compare with the compounds we found on the McGee boy so I'll be able to confirm it for you. The team is also swabbing the entire boat for the victim's DNA to fully tie it down."

Angus turned to face Murphy again.

"Thanks, Murphy. Great job. I feel like I owe you."

"A cup of coffee will do, Sheriff. All you have to do is ask." She threw him a sideways smile before she turned to instruct her team to wrap up her investigation.

"Now go do your job, Sheriff, and catch the guy who killed our guy over here." She winked as she said it.

Angus made an amused salute in reply before he left the boat and got behind the wheel of his car, its nose headed straight toward Raymond McGee's trailer at the edge of town.

"But whoever drinks of the water that I shall give him will never thirst. But the water that I shall give him will become in him a fountain of water springing up into everlasting life."

John 4:14

Angus Reid's journey continues in **the second Angus Reid Mystery novel,** where more will be revealed! (SNEAK A PEEK! READ ON!)

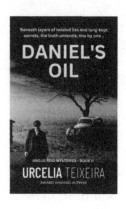

Mystery runs deep in Weyport when Patty Richardson suddenly finds herself knee-deep in a secret that lies far closer to her than she'd ever thought possible.

Save when you get it at Urcelia Teixeira's online shop!! (https://shop.urcelia.com)

GET DANIEL'S OIL (books.urcelia.com/Daniels-Oil)

Want updates? Join my Reader Community (newsletter.urcelia.com/signup)

Thank you for reading *JACOB'S WELL*. I hope you loved getting to know Sheriff Angus Reid as much as I did. I pray God touched you in a special way that drew you into a more intimate relationship with Him as He did me while I studied the scriptures that inspired this story. **Please consider leaving a review so others might hear this message too.**

TURN THE PAGE TO START READING DANIEL'S OIL

Beneath layers of twisted lies and long-kept
secrets, the truth unravels, one by one...

DANIEL'S OIL

ANGUS REID MYSTERIES - BOOK II

URCELIA TEIXEIRA

AWARD WINNING AUTHOR

DANIEL'S OIL

A TWISTY CHRISTIAN MYSTERY NOVEL

ANGUS REID MYSTERIES BOOK II

URCELIA TEIXEIRA

Copyrighted material
E-book © ISBN: 978-1-928537-90-8
Regular Print Paperback © ISBN: 978-1-928537-91-5
Large Print Paperback © ISBN: 978-1-928537-92-2
Published by Purpose Bound Press
Written by Urcelia Teixeira   Edited by Perfect Pages Editor
First edition
Urcelia Teixeira
Wiltshire, UK
https://www.urcelia.com

Love may forgive all infirmities and love still in spite of them: but love cannot cease to will their removal.

C. S. Lewis

INSPIRED BY

"Do not remember the former things,
nor consider the things of old..."
Isaiah 43:18
(NKJV)

PREFACE

She should have known. The signs were there, right under her nose, plain as day. Only now, she's meant to look the other way. Bury the pain and the shame as if nothing ever happened.

But, instead, what has rooted is the fine line between hate and forgiveness, torturing her soul with questions forever left unanswered.

And that is the most treacherous tightrope of all...

CHAPTER ONE

D aniel Richardson always knew his choice would carry risks. That his decision on that fateful night would haunt him for decades to come. But that night, at that moment, when the entire building of his life was threatened to be ripped down to the studs, he had told himself that having a choice was not his to enjoy. That there was no other way. That he could live with his conscience. Until the day he died.

And, as time passed, he learned to ignore the still voices within. The ones that nagged with guilt and shame, and sometimes niggled with regret. He knew it was never going to be easy, but now, nearly two decades on, his secret had rooted and buried itself deep into the layers and fibers of his identity to where it had become hardly noticeable.

Even to himself.

Except he had never properly considered how heavy

the weight of his decision would be. No matter how hard he hid the events of that night from himself, he hadn't taken into account that the real work lay with swaying the conscience of those who knew his secret.

PUSHING INTROSPECTION ASIDE, Daniel hastened down the hallway to their small foyer, as his wife's voice came from the sitting room behind him.

"I don't know why you still bother going to these silly town hall meetings. You're only making a fool of yourself," Patty said, where from behind her evening cup of tea she watched her husband get ready to leave.

He briefly glanced at her, knowing the true intent veiled by her words. What she implied was that he was making a fool of *her*.

"They're not silly to me, Patty. I have a vested interest in the buildings in this town and you know it. Keep in mind I built half of these buildings and it's my duty to make sure we maintain the standards that make Weyport a great place to live."

He slipped on his brown trench coat along with his matching tweed newsboy cap, which he shifted in place at the back of his head.

"Had, Daniel, had. You are retired, remember? Your days of having a *vested* interest in what construction goes on in this town are long gone. You really should leave it to the younger generation to decide what needs building and what doesn't. It's not as if we will be around forever to enjoy it, you know."

Daniel grunted as he shot his wife of forty-five years a sideways glance that conveyed his frustration with her comments.

He pulled his hat down over his eyes before he turned to face her.

"It's thanks to hardworking people like my grandfather and me that there *is* a town this *younger* generation might enjoy. They don't know the first thing about the building trade. Everything's on computers and half the materials they use are cheap substitutes. My grandfather taught me everything he knew and quality—"

"Yada, yada, yada, family business. I know, Daniel. No one knows the trade better than you. I've heard it all a thousand times before, but times have changed, and the industry is transforming faster than you can say *build me a house*. I mean look at you, wearing your grandfather's cap and coat like you are clinging to your younger years. It's ridiculous. Your grandfather is long gone, and you closed the doors to the family business the day you retired eight years ago. It's high time you accept your age and fill your days with more important things. Like going to church."

Daniel shot her another glare as his hand reached for the doorknob.

"Don't wait up," he mumbled over his shoulder and pulled the front door shut behind him.

When he stepped off the porch, the rain drenched his

coat before he bridged the few yards to his car. He slipped behind the wheel of his tomato red BMW. His midlife crisis vehicle, as Patty had dubbed it when he first pulled up the drive in it shortly after his fiftieth birthday. It was just another thing for which she had shown her disdain. But eighteen years of her ceaseless complaining about it had long since been shelved, along with the rest of her fault-finding that he had learned to ignore over the years.

Irritation settled in his spirit. Patricia Richardson might have been his wife on paper but that was all. She had never truly understood or respected him like a proper wife should have, he mused. Sure, in the early years of marriage their relationship was great. But somewhere around the halfway mark he had seen her respect for him fade with her return from each Country Club tennis game or women's tea she attended. His thoughts continued spiraling downward. It was so typical of her, thinking she was somehow above him and the blue-collar town hall meetings, as she called them . As if her fancy women's luncheons and pretentious church meetings somehow elevated her rite of passage through life. A spoiled banker's daughter who never had any admiration for him or his profession.

As a fresh wave of rain splashed in his face, Daniel slammed the car's door. He pushed the car into gear and hastily backed out of the driveway, his mood as dark and thunderous as the evening sky.

"Stupid woman," he said aloud, as if Patty had something to do with the weather.

DRIVING OFF, he shifted his mind to keeping the car on the road instead. The windshield wipers were already at full speed and seeing the road ahead became increasingly difficult in the heavy downpour. After a longer drive than usual, he parked in front of the town hall. As always, he was on time but rushed inside nonetheless. He had always taken great pride in being punctual.

Just inside the entrance of the town hall, he pulled his wet cap from his head and tucked it in his coat's side pocket, he slipped his coat off, and draped the wet garment over one arm.

"It's quite the storm out tonight isn't it, Mr. Richardson? Do you want me to take that for you?" A young woman from the mayor's office held her hands out to take his coat, eyeing the small puddles it was leaving all over the floor.

"No need, it's just water. Nothing your diligent hands can't manage I'm sure," Daniel mumbled grumpily.

He snatched up the meeting agenda from the entry table and made his way to his regular aisle seat in the third row and draped his wet coat over the open chair next to him to keep anyone from sitting in it. The hall soon filled up around him and with a slight tip of the head he acknowledged a few passing tradesmen. When he had had enough of the pleasantries he turned his attention to the piece of paper in his hand and pored over the evening's agenda. His eyes fell on the first entry and traced the line item with his callused forefinger, grunting under his breath when he read the name assigned to it.

Shifting uncomfortably in his chair, he looked up and searched the faces until he found who he was looking for.

CHAPTER TWO

Bill Baxter's eyes locked with Daniel's, lingered on his face, and then quickly looked away.

Coward, Daniel thought, dreading having to listen to whatever it was Bill had to contribute to the night's agenda. He had managed to avoid the man for years but just seeing him schmoozing with the mayor made his blood boil. Knowing Bill Baxter, he had something up his dirty sleeve.

"Judging from that frosty look I see the two of you are still at it," Caleb Townsend said as he took the seat diagonally behind Daniel and draped his hands over the back of Daniel's coat chair.

"The man's a greedy weasel," Daniel replied. "Honestly, I don't know how you can stomach working with him. I'm sure one of those big conveyance firms in Boston

267

would snatch you up in a heartbeat if you went knocking on one of their doors."

"Bill's not that bad. Besides, I like Weyport, and I can't really do without his business. Best to keep him sweet, if you know what I mean," Caleb joked.

"Yeah, I'd watch my back if I were you." Daniel paused then continued. "I didn't realize your business was struggling, considering you're the only conveyance attorney in town and all. Business should be booming."

Caleb snickered.

"Take a good look around, Daniel. These people make up the entire property trade in Weyport and most of us are still trying to recover from the whole Covid-19 debacle. New construction pretty much dried up and there are not many property sales happening at the moment either. Haven't been for a while now. Without more development and expansion, it's a matter of time before I'll be forced to shut my firm's doors. And my legal expertise can only stomach so many re-mortgages and deed claims."

Daniel's eyes narrowed as he paused to study Caleb's face.

"Bill sent you to soften me up, didn't he?"

Caleb didn't answer.

"That's what this is about. I should have known some-thing was up the minute I saw his name on the agenda. You playing the pity card is supposed to pave the way for him. Is this about that stupid lake proposal of his? Tell me,

Caleb, when did you become one of Bill Baxter's puppets, huh?"

"I'm no one's puppet, Daniel, but let's face it. Weyport needs the business. More and more families are moving down from the city. This town was bound to grow out of space. There simply aren't enough homes to go around. And if his proposal for the luxury development by the lake is approved, we all win. The entire town wins."

Daniel turned to look at him.

"Over my dead body," he replied. "The ground adjacent to the lake isn't sound for building and Bill knows it."

"There are ways around that, Daniel. With proper drainage and sound foundations, it should be fine."

"All of which will take time and a lot of engineering costs to properly execute. You and I both know Bill Baxter's only goal is to get his houses done as fast as possible so he can get his money and move on to the next quick buck. My family built the very foundations of this town and I will not sit by and watch that man smear my name through the mud. It's not going to happen as long as I have a say in this and you can take that back to Bill to choke on."

Daniel was already up on his feet.

Caleb stood up too.

"What happened between the two of you, Daniel? You used to be friends. Heck the two of you practically built Weyport together. Why do you hate Bill so much?"

Caleb's clever trump card stabbed at something deep inside but Daniel quickly stifled his emotions.

"That man is a lying crook, Caleb, cheating people out of their hard earned money by selling them homes that aren't up to code. You should be ashamed of yourself. Unless of course he's got you in his back pocket to keep your firm afloat."

Daniel's eyes narrowed as he waited for Caleb to respond to his accusation, but he never did. Instead, Caleb turned away and joined Bill and a few of the other board members where they were huddled together in deep conversation on the other side of the room.

"The cheek," Daniel muttered under his breath as he snatched his coat from the chair and made for the door.

But, by the time he reached the end of the aisle, Bill Baxter's voice boomed through the microphone.

Murmurs in the crowded town hall dwindled and Daniel paused in the doorway, curiosity overcoming his desire to storm out.

"Ladies and gentlemen," Bill began, his voice dripping with a false charm that wormed its way under Daniel's skin.

"I have an exciting announcement to share tonight," Bill continued as the room fell into an expectant hush. All eyes turned toward the podium where Bill stood in all his six foot five inch glory, sporting a grin so wide it made Daniel's stomach turn.

Across the hall, Daniel's gaze locked with Bill's, a mixture of suspicion and apprehension in his eyes.

"As you all know," Bill continued, "Weyport has been experiencing a housing shortage for quite some time now. City families who long to make Weyport their new home are moving in at a rapid pace and are struggling to find suitable homes. With the growing demand, we at Weyport Realty have come up with a solution—a ground-breaking property development that will give this town a much needed boost!"

Daniel watched as a wave of excitement rippled through a large portion of the crowd while others stirred with skepticism. He crossed his arms and raised his chin, sending a clear signal to Bill that he was ready to counter his proposal with all his might.

Bill cleared his throat and continued.

"I propose the construction of a state-of-the-art housing estate on the land south of the lake."

He paused and pointed to a slide projected on a large screen behind him. "This development will not only provide both luxury and affordable housing for current and new residents, but it will also generate a substantial revenue to our town's business community. Not to mention that it will, without a doubt, provide much needed new jobs."

Murmurs of approval and dissent echoed through the room as people absorbed Bill's sales pitch.

"What about the concerns regarding the ground? It's

bordering the wetland. Do we really need a repeat of what happened before?" someone from the crowd called out.

Daniel grunted his concurrence.

But Bill flashed a confident smile. "That was a very long time ago and, rest assured, new technology has given us the opportunity to conduct extensive studies. We were able to acquire surveys from some of the country's best engineers and have come up with ways to address that very issue. I guarantee you that all the necessary measures will be taken to ensure the absolute safety of both workers and prospective residents. Once completed, this project will provide a significant shift for Weyport."

As Bill continued, Daniel watched as more questions were thrown Bill's way. But the man had a clever answer for every single one. Daniel's fists clenched tighter across his chest as rage swept through him. This was one project he could not afford to move forward.

Not now, not ever.

CHAPTER THREE

I t wasn't long before Bill's practiced charm worked its magic with the attendees as the atmosphere turned into one of celebration, as if the project had already gotten the all clear.

It was as if Bill Baxter had put the town in a trance as they were fixed onto his every lie.

Daniel watched in irritation from the back of the room where he had quietly slipped into an open seat. Apart from a handful of keen birdwatchers expressing their concern over the neighboring wetlands, most of the people around him had fully bought into the project by the lake. Even the mayor showed his support by patting Bill on his back and shaking his hand. The gatherers cheered and clapped as they shouted congratulatory praises at Bill, as if the man was some kind of saint who came to save Weyport.

Nauseating disgust rose in Daniel's throat as bitterness and rage took over his insides.

Bill Baxter had done it. He had won them over, pulled the wool over their eyes like he had always done, and there was not a single thing Daniel could do about it.

He got to his feet and made for the door, briefly looking back over his shoulder at Bill who was relishing in his premature victory. Bill caught Daniel looking and gave him a gloating grin before he continued lapping up the attention with the rest of his presentation.

The rain beat down on Daniel's car as he pushed its nose back home, nearly veering off the road when he took a corner too fast. But the wicked weather was no match for what raged within. This was no longer about Bill winning the hand, or even the smug look on his face when he rubbed his victory in Daniel's face. Nor did any of it have anything to do with his grandfather's legacy.

What had Daniel Richardson's skin tingling and his stomach in knots, was what he had spent the last eighteen years covering up.

WHEN HIS CAR screeched to a halt in his driveway, Patty's face appeared from behind the lace drapes in the window, her eyes squinting into his car's headlights. By the time he reached the porch, she already had the front door open and he stormed in.

"Back so soon? I thought you told me not to wait up."

He slammed the door behind him.

"Not now, Patty," he yelled and flung his wet coat and hat on the coat stand.

"What's gotten into you? Why are you storming in here, looking like this?"

"I said not now, Patty. I don't want to talk about it."

But Patty had gotten to know her husband's moods over the nearly fifty years they had been together. There was only one man in Weyport who could have put her husband in such a foul mood.

"Let me guess. You had a run in with Bill Baxter again, didn't you?" She had the mop in hand and headed for the muddy puddles he had left in his wake. "I don't want to say it, but I told you so. You don't need to be at these meetings anymore," she continued.

"That man's going to be the death of me! He's got this entire town wrapped around his dirty little finger as if he owns it."

Patty set the mop down.

"Out with it then. What has the guy done now that has you this agitated?"

"He's proposing to build one of his second-rate developments on the property by the lake. He had the whole town eating from his hand before his stupid presentation was through. Everyone knows the ground isn't stable and yet they're cheering him on as if he's saving the world. It's ridiculous."

"And what's so bad about that? It's high time Weyport expands. Not to mention all the jobs he'd be creating."

Daniel stood facing his wife, his face as red as his car.

"Don't tell me you're agreeing with this! My grandfather's name—"

"Oh, spare me the spiel about your precious family name, Daniel. As if you honestly care. You cannot possibly be opposed to this. That land by the lake has been standing empty since before you were even born. It's prime property and it makes complete sense to be used for development. What's not to like? The views would be spectacular, and this town could do with the additional revenue it would bring in. I think this is less about the land and more about your ego."

Daniel stared at his wife, the veins in his temples pulsing with indignation.

"I don't know why I thought you would support me on this. You have never supported me on anything. It's like you intentionally push against me just for the sake of it. I should have expected you'd be on his side along with all the other traitors in this town."

He turned and stormed off to the bedroom, Patty trailing in his wake.

"Then help me understand you, Daniel. What's so bad about using the land next to the lake to build a few new homes?"

"The man is a crook, Patty. The land isn't safe. But he conveniently weaseled his way out of that question when someone else who had a bit of sense asked him about it tonight. Bill cuts corners. He's not concerned about people's safety or how this town would supposedly prosper. All he cares about is himself and how much money he'll be adding to his private bank account."

Patty studied her husband's face.

"Why don't you offer to help him then? If it's about building up to code and keeping people safe, why don't you offer to consult and make sure he follows the best practices."

Daniel's eyes turned even darker.

"Over my dead body. I will never work with that man ever again. Never! Do you hear me, Patty? I want nothing to do with Bill Baxter or anything he touches. Mark my words. Nothing good will come from this. Nothing!"

He snatched his pajamas from his closet and stormed down the hall before he disappeared into the guest bedroom, slamming the door shut behind him.

DISBELIEF over her husband's angry outburst and the hatred he had shown toward Bill left Patty confused when she climbed into bed. Daniel had always been short tempered, and a grouch if she were to call a spade a spade. But in all the years they had been married, she'd never seen that much animosity pour from him.

Was there something else that lurked behind his tantrum?

Suspicion prodded at her insides as she tossed in bed. It wasn't like him to not want to see a home take shape, even if it wasn't built according to housing code. Creating homes was his passion. It was as if with each new construction he had given birth to a child, welcoming it into purpose.

But tonight, she had seen something different in her husband's eyes. Hidden behind dark clouds as if it had been brewing there for many years. If she didn't know her husband any better, she could have sworn she saw fear. A desperate kind of fear. And it left her uncomfortable and, dared she say, scared.

Yes, she thought as she drifted off to sleep, Daniel's opposition to the project by the lake was masking something far more important. Something important enough that he would rather die than give way to it.

But the lingering question that played at the back of her mind was how far would Daniel Richardson go to keep pretending he cared more about his family legacy and the safety of the land at the lake than what truly lay hidden behind his fear.

She would challenge him on it tomorrow and get to the truth. Even if he never spoke to her again.

CHAPTER FOUR

A s always, Patty woke up at four a.m. When she passed the guest room on the way to the kitchen, she lingered outside the door to listen for Daniel's soft snores. She had grown quite used to his gentle snoring, lulling her to sleep every night and she had oddly missed his presence the night before.

When she didn't hear him, she pressed her ear harder against the door. Remorse for the part she had in the previous night's events suddenly tugged at her heart and her finger gently traced the doorknob. Twenty years ago, she would have playfully slipped into bed with him. But things between them were different now. Distant. Over all the years they had been married, they had only ever slept in separate rooms a handful of times - usually when he came home late from his game of bridge and didn't want to wake her. But mostly, they didn't sleep in separate rooms because they were both too stubborn to give up the bedroom when they had had a spat.

She'd make it up to him, she thought, as she continued into the kitchen to brew the morning pot of coffee. He would not be up until his usual time of eight o'clock when he would expect to sit down to the wholesome breakfast he had insisted was the least of her wifely duties. Then all spats would be forgotten, as if no hurtful words were ever spoken between them the night before.

A slight smile curled at the corners of her mouth as she recalled her late mother once telling her that it was a special gift only men possessed. Over the years, her mother's words were proven to be right more times than she could count.

Forgiveness usually came easy to her so the decision to make him his favorite breakfast was a quick one.

She took her cup of coffee to the dining table where she had gotten into the daily habit of reading her Bible and writing in her journal.

But when she pulled back the lace window covering and glanced out into the street which was part of her morning ritual, her eyes fell upon the empty space in their drive.

At first, she thought her eyes were playing tricks on her but when she looked more closely at the spot where Daniel's car should have been, there was no mistaking it.

His car was gone.

"Thieves!" she blurted out in annoyance, thinking it

must have been stolen since the neighborhood had had an increase in burglaries of late.

She hurried over to the phone and was about to lift it to her ear when she thought it best to let Daniel report the incident instead.

She started calling out to him as she hurried down the hall, briefly knocking on the door before she burst into the guest room.

"Daniel, the thugs who have been going around the neighborhood stole your car," she blurted out and reached for the light switch next to her.

As the room lit up, her eyes found the bed empty, the bedspread neatly in place indicating he hadn't slept in the bed at all.

She nervously glanced at her small gold wristwatch. He was never up that early.

"Daniel?" She called out toward the bathroom then walked into their bedroom on the off chance he crawled back in bed and she hadn't noticed.

After she had searched every room in the house and did not find him, it was clear her husband's vehicle was never stolen and that he must have left after she went to bed the night before.

THE EARLY MORNING sunrise cast its golden rays across the calm waters of the lake and transformed it into a shimmering surface that lit up like a giant mirror in the middle of the expansive stretch of land. Grateful that it had stopped raining a few hours after he got there the night before, Daniel dropped the spade on the firm sand next to his feet then knelt beside it. With the back of his sleeve, he wiped his face as he stared out across the basin. In the distance, the wetland birdlife was starting to come to life, descending on the lake where they scooped down and grabbed their early morning catch. Under a furrowed brow, his eyes surveyed the parts of land he hadn't yet searched, and his shoulders dropped even lower. It was simply too much ground to cover. Years ago he had used the river gauge as his marker but it had somehow disappeared, likely due to rising water levels or storms that had passed through the area over the years. Without the marker it would take him days, longer if he could only search at night.

And time was not on his side.

He squinted into the soft morning light as doubt and fear settled in. Perhaps he was on the wrong side of the lake. It had been so long since he had last been there and his memory wasn't what it used to be. Everything about that night had become fuzzy.

He cursed between tight lips. He should have destroyed it. That night, or the next day even. It was a foolish oversight when his nerves got the better of him. Or perhaps he was tempting fate and wanted to die too. At the very least, he should have written the location down, or drawn a map. He would have been able to find it by now and destroy it, doing what he should have done all those years ago. Before his past finally caught up to him.

But, as Daniel sat there, contemplating his mistakes, it dawned on him that if he couldn't find it, there was a good chance no one else would either. And with any luck, the housing development would never happen, at least not while he was still alive.

He pushed himself off the damp soil that had soaked his pants and dirtied most of his cream-colored shirt. He had been at it all night and, at sixty-eight years of age, his body wasn't accustomed to that much physical exertion anymore. Exhausted, he groaned when he stood upright, his body aching in places he had long forgotten to exercise. He had left his car on the edge of the land and walked toward it, casting a watchful eye in every direction—just in case an early dog walker or fisherman surprised him. From the passenger side of his car, he slipped into the front seat and took his pewter hip flask from the glovebox. It was one more item of his grandfather's he had held onto. Putting the small spout to his lips, the strong liquor burned his dry throat as he drank two mouthfuls before he closed it back inside the cubby. If Patty were there, she would have thrown her scriptures at him.

It was nearly seven thirty. He had to get going before someone saw him. For now, he would leave it be. Who knew, perhaps Patty's God would extend some of that mercy she was always going on about his way and keep his secret buried under the sand forever.

He walked around to the driver's side and dropped in behind the wheel, resting his dirty hands on the steering wheel as he stared out across the land in front of him.

"It's going to be fine, Daniel Richardson," he told himself out loud. "It'll all be all right."

If he had managed to keep it a secret for this long, why would he worry about it now? Besides, there were only three people in the entire world who knew the truth and two of them were dead.

CHAPTER FIVE

Patty restlessly paced the small space of her kitchen. Perhaps Daniel had finally decided to leave her. Perhaps their strained relationship over the past two decades had finally pushed him to quit their marriage.

Her mother had warned her of the fine line between independence and submissiveness in marriage. Daniel was old-school; his expectations of a wife were precisely the opposite of who she was. He wanted her to be reserved, to support him no matter what. *He* needed to be the one to shine, be the king of his castle. And heaven knew she had never been able to do that. Her daddy had raised her to be an independent woman, one who stood proudly and could voice her own opinions. Patty was many things, but she was never the timid little wife Daniel had always wanted. Nor was she able to give him the son he so desperately needed to carry on his family's business. They tried for years but it was as if her body rejected the duty of bearing an heir to his family lineage. And that was the biggest disappointment of all.

She placed her empty coffee cup in the kitchen sink and was ready to store away the delicious salmon omelette she had specially cooked for Daniel when she heard his key in the front door.

Her heart leapt inside her chest as she walked towards the foyer.

Daniel tossed his damp coat onto the coat stand and took off his shoes, clumps of dirt falling to the floor around him.

When he looked up at Patty there was a strange look in his eyes, one that almost looked apologetic, yet he didn't utter a word.

"Is everything all right, Daniel?" Patty asked as her eyes inspected his dirty clothing.

"Fine. I'm going to take a shower."

"There's breakfast. I made you your favorite. Salmon omelette, the nice Norwegian one you like."

"I'm not hungry." He pushed past her, disappearing into their bedroom.

Stunned, Patty's gaze turned back to his coat and shoes and the taupe colored dirt that now covered the hardwood floor.

Fetching the broom and dustpan in the kitchen her mind raced with questions. But none more curious than the ones that arose when she swept the clusters of damp sand into the dustpan. From experience, she knew it wasn't beach sand. Nor was it the dirt that had clung to his work boots when he returned home from a build.

She rubbed a few grains between her fingers as her mind worked through the possibilities.

"What are you doing?" Daniel's sudden presence startled her and she jumped up.

"Cleaning the mess you made, that's all."

"Are you spying on me?"

"No, why would I be doing that? Unless you have something to hide, of course."

She moved past him into the kitchen, her insides bursting to ask him where he had been.

Daniel made a grunting sound and when she realized he was heading back out the door, she hurried toward the foyer.

"Where are you going?" she asked. "You just got here."

"What's with all the questions, huh, Patty? Don't you have one of your feminist meetings to go to?"

His words stung but she wasn't going to let it go.

"Where were you last night, Daniel? And what's with all the dirt all over your shoes and clothing?"

Daniel scoffed. "Since when do you have any interest in what I'm up to? What business is it of yours where I go? The last time I checked you couldn't give a hoot what I do so save me the false concern. You're just looking for another story to take to your high society gossip queens."

He pulled his hat in place at the back of his head.

Hurt lay shallow in the hollow of her throat as she watched him and, with one hand clutching at the invisible pearls around her neck, Patty swallowed hard to hold back her tears.

"That's not true, Daniel. I was worried."

He scoffed.

"I would never betray you. I am still your wife."

"Really? Are you sure about that, Patty? Because last night you picked Bill Baxter's side."

"I didn't pick his side. I was merely trying to get you to open up to me."

"You could have fooled me. You defended him, even told me to offer my expertise to the man. That's the most ridiculous thing I've ever heard and you, of all people, should know better."

"What's going on, Daniel? Where were you last night?"

Daniel didn't answer.

"Why are you shutting me out? If it's about this business with the lake, maybe I can help. The Women's League is meeting—"

"Women's League! There you go again. Always thinking you have all the answers and all the influence. I don't need you to fly in and take over. I am quite capable of handling this without your self-claimed women power."

"I didn't mean it that way, I just...don't go, Daniel. We can work this out."

Daniel looked at her sideways.

"You stopped being my wife many years ago, Patty. Your choice, not mine."

He turned toward the door and left without saying another word, leaving Patty to stand in the middle of the hallway clutching her throat.

She had had every intention of apologizing to her husband and smoothing things over. But this time, this time his words cut far too deep, and Patty could no longer control the tears that now ran freely down her cheeks.

WHEN BILL BAXTER walked into a room the entire room sat up straight. He had a certain authoritative air about him that made people pay attention to him. Tall, with broad shoulders, and slightly overweight around the midriff, he walked into the mayor's office.

"You're still smiling. That's a good sign," he said as the mayor stood to shake his hand.

"Why wouldn't I? This project is just what Weyport needs in the wake of an economic downturn. A little pick-me-up to make this town of ours even greater," the mayor said as they walked to the boardroom.

"Yeah, I would be lying if I said I wasn't excited," Bill said as he accepted a cup of coffee from the mayor's assistant.

"So come on then, my friend. Don't keep me in

suspense. Show me the blueprints so we can get this thing going," the mayor prompted.

Bill spread the sheets of rolled up paper across the boardroom table, weighing them down on the corners with coffee cups. He spent the following fifteen minutes going over the finer details of the soil compounds and the findings of the German engineering team with whom he had been consulting.

The mayor shook his head in amazement.

"I don't know why you didn't think to develop that piece of land a long time ago, Bill. It's going to be an exceptional residential development when you are done with it. Whatever you need from me to help you get this done, just say the word. Permits, road closures, you name it."

Bill's hands went to his hips.

"I appreciate that, Mr. Mayor, but getting permits signed is the least of my concerns."

Curiosity lit up the mayor's eyes.

"Daniel Richardson," Bill informed.

"What about him?" the mayor asked, looking confused.

"He owns the adjacent land and a substantial piece of it cuts directly across the proposed building site." His fingers pointed to a large area on the blueprints. "We've tried every which way we could to work around it but with the soil challenges and so forth, we just can't go ahead without it. We stand to lose about forty percent of the total project revenue, which shoots our profit margins straight out of the water. The project won't be financially viable without encompassing that particular piece of land."

"And he wouldn't sell it?"

"Have you met Daniel Richardson? There's not a chance of him selling, ever! He would rather die than sell it, much less to me. That piece of land belonged to his grandfather and clinging onto his family's legacy means everything to him. He will never let it go."

ENJOYED THE SNEAK PEEK? **ONE-CLICK** TO READ WHAT HAPPENS NEXT!

MORE BOOKS BY URCELIA TEIXEIRA

Angus Reid Mysteries series
Jacob's Well
Daniel's Oil
Caleb's Cross

Adam Cross series
Every Good Gift
Every Good Plan
Every Good Work

Jorja Rose trilogy
Vengeance is Mine
Shadow of Fear
Wages of Sin

Alex Hunt series
The Papua Incident (FREE!)
The Rhapta Key
The Gilded Treason
The Alpha Strain
The Dauphin Deception
The Bari Bones
The Caiaphas Code

PICK A BUNDLE FOR MASSIVE SAVINGS exclusive to my online
store!
Save up to 50% off plus get an additional 10% discount coupon.
Visit https://shop.urcelia.com

More books coming soon! Sign up to my newsletter to be notified of new releases, giveaways and pre-release specials.

MESSAGE FROM THE AUTHOR

All glory be to the Lord, my God who breathed every word through me onto these pages.

*I have put my words in your mouth and
covered you with the shadow of My hand
Isaiah 51:16*

It is my sincere prayer that you not only enjoyed the story, but drew courage, inspiration, and hope from it, just as I did while writing it. Thank you sincerely, for reading *JACOB'S WELL*.

**I appreciate your help in spreading the word,
including telling a friend. Reviews help
readers find books! Please leave a review on
your favorite book site.**

ABOUT THE AUTHOR

Award winning author of faith-filled Christian Suspense Thrillers that won't let you go!™

Urcelia Teixeira, writes gripping Christian mystery, thriller and suspense novels that will keep you on the edge of your seat! Firm in her Christian faith, all her books are free from profanity and unnecessary sexually suggestive scenes.

She made her writing debut in December 2017, kicking off her newly discovered author journey with her fast-paced archaeological adventure thriller novels that readers have described as 'Indiana Jones meets Lara Croft with a twist of Bourne.'

But, five novels in, and nearly eighteen months later, she had a spiritual re-awakening, and she wrote the sixth and final book in her Alex Hunt Adventure Thriller series. She now fondly refers to *The Caiaphas Code* as her redemption book. Her statement of faith. And although this series has reached multiple Amazon Bestseller lists, she took the bold step of following her true calling and switched to writing what honors her Creator: Christian Mystery and Suspense fiction.

The first book in her newly discovered genre went on to win the 2021 Illumination Awards Silver medal in the Christian Fiction category and the series reached multiple Amazon Bestseller lists!

While this success is a great honor and blessing, all glory goes to God alone who breathed every word through her!

A committed Christian for over twenty years, she now lives by the following mantra:

"I used to be a writer. Now I am a writer with a purpose!"

For more on Urcelia and her books, visit https://www.urcelia.com

To walk alongside her as she deepens her writing journey and walks with God, sign up to her Newsletter - https://newsletter.urcelia.com/signup

or

Follow her at

goodreads.com/urcelia_teixeira

facebook.com/urceliateixeira

bookbub.com/authors/urcelia-teixeira

amazon.com/author/urceliateixeira

instagram.com/urceliateixeira

pinterest.com/urcelia_teixeira

Made in the USA
Monee, IL
17 December 2023

49128409R00184